Wa

D0052128

Jennie Lucas

ITALIAN PRINCE, WEDLOCKED WIFE

HARLEQUIN®
Presents

Welcome to the January 2009 collection of Harlequin Presents!

This month be sure to catch the second installment of Lynne Graham's trilogy VIRGIN BRIDES, ARROGANT HUSBANDS with her new book, *The Ruthless Magnate's Virgin Mistress*. Jessica goes from office cleaner to the billionaire boss's mistress in Sharon Kendrick's *Bought for the Sicilian Billionaire's Bed*, and sexual attraction simmers uncontrollably when Tara has to face the ruthless count in *Count Maxime's Virgin* by Susan Stephens. You'll be whisked off to the Mediterranean in Michelle Reid's *The Greek's Forced Bride*, and in Jennie Lucas's *Italian Prince, Wedlocked Wife*, innocent Lucy tries to resist the seductive ways of Prince Maximo. A ruthless tycoon will stop at nothing to bed his convenient wife in Anne McAllister's *Antonides' Forbidden Wife*, and friends become lovers when playboy Alex Richardson needs a bride in Kate Hardy's *Hotly Bedded, Conveniently Wedded*. Plus, in Trish Wylie's *Claimed by the Rogue Billionaire*, attraction reaches the boiling point between Gabe and Ash, but can either of them forget the past?

We'd love to hear what you think about Presents. E-mail us at Presents@hmb.co.uk or join in the discussions at www.iheartpresents.com and www.sensationalromance.blogspot.com, where you'll also find more information about books and authors!

RED HOT REVENGE

There are times in a man's life...
when only seduction will settle old scores!

Pick up our exciting series of revenge-filled
romances—they're recommended and red-hot!

Available only from Harlequin Presents®

Jennie Lucas

ITALIAN PRINCE, WEDLOCKED WIFE

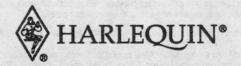

TORONTO • NEW YORK • LONDON
AMSTERDAM • PARIS • SYDNEY • HAMBURG
STOCKHOLM • ATHENS • TOKYO • MILAN • MADRID
PRAGUE • WARSAW • BUDAPEST • AUCKLAND

ISBN-13: 978-0-373-12790-0
ISBN-10: 0-373-12790-1

ITALIAN PRINCE, WEDLOCKED WIFE

First North American Publication 2009.

All about the author...
Jennie Lucas

JENNIE LUCAS had a tragic beginning for any would-be writer: a very happy childhood. Her parents owned a bookstore, and she grew up surrounded by books, dreaming about faraway lands. When she was ten, her father secretly paid her a dollar for every classic novel (*Jane Eyre, War and Peace*) that she read.

At fifteen, she went to a Connecticut boarding school on scholarship. She took her first solo trip to Europe at sixteen, then put off college and traveled around the U.S., supporting herself with jobs as diverse as gas-station cashier and newspaper advertising assistant.

At twenty-two, she met the man who would be her husband. For the first time in her life, she wanted to stay in one place, as long as she could be with him. After their marriage, she graduated from Kent State University with a degree in English, and she started writing books a year later.

Jennie was a finalist in the Romance Writers of America Golden Heart contest in 2003, and won the award in 2005. A fellow 2003 finalist, Australian author Trish Morey, read Jennie's writing and told her that she should write for Harlequin Presents. It seemed like too big a dream, but Jennie took a deep breath and went for it. A year later Jennie got the magical call from London that turned her into a published author.

Since then, life has been hectic—she's juggling a writing career, a sexy husband and two young children—but Jennie loves her crazy, chaotic life. Now if she could only figure out how to pack her family up and live in all the places she's writing about...

For more about Jennie and her books, please visit her Web site at www.jennielucas.com.

To Anna Marie Allen,
Aunti *par excellence*—
I couldn't have written this book without you.

CHAPTER ONE

HE'D found her!

Prince Maximo d'Aquilla parked his Mercedes beneath a broken streetlight, staring at the brightly lit gas station. The shining light from the shop's windows illuminated the snowy night like a flame in the darkness, silhouetting the girl working alone inside.

Lucia Ferrazzi.

The granddaughter of his enemy. The ex-lover of his business rival.

Fate, he thought, gripping the steering wheel. *Il destino*. After all these years of looking, how else to explain it?

His phone rang. Ermanno, one of the bodyguards waiting in the car parked behind him, said a single word: *"Signore?"*

"Wait for my signal," Maximo replied in Italian, and snapped his phone shut.

He watched her for another five minutes. It was ten o'clock on New Year's Eve, and the store should have been busy selling wine and beer; but the run-down

South Chicago neighborhood was eerily dark and deserted beneath the heavily falling snow.

The girl assisted her only customer at the cash register with a shy smile. Her scrubbed, clean face made her seem younger than twenty-one, he thought. Cat's-eye glasses framed her wide-set brown eyes, giving her plain features a dowdy, bookish look.

She would fall to him easily, he thought.

The solitary customer left, and a gray sedan skidded to a stop near the gas pumps. A thin man stepped out of the car. He stared at the girl, spraying breath freshener into his mouth, then started toward the store.

Maximo saw the alarm in the girl's eyes, the way she bit her tender pink lip as she watched the slender man come toward the door. She was afraid of him.

Maximo allowed himself a single, grim smile. She didn't realize how much her world had changed.

As of now, she was under Maximo's protection.

Before the clock struck midnight, she would be his bride.

His revenge would be complete. And as for that other matter…

He pushed the thought firmly from his mind. It would all be over. He would take her, and in three months, he'd be free. Free—of everything.

"Oh, no," Lucy Abbott whispered aloud. The sound of her voice echoed in the empty store.

She leaned her head against the glass, watching as her smarmy manager came toward the door. She'd prayed she wouldn't see him tonight. That he would have a date, a party, *anything* to keep him from stopping by to "check on the store."

Just one more week, she reminded herself with a deep breath. One more week to put up with Darryl's crude jokes, the way he stared at her breasts beneath her cashier's smock, the way he would "accidentally" brush his groin against her hip amid the narrow aisles of chips and candy.

She'd applied to be an assistant manager at a nearby store, and she needed his good reference until her position was finalized next week. Then Lucy could say goodbye to him forever. And even better, she would get a raise. For the first time since her baby had been born, she would be able to have just one job instead of three—she could work just forty hours a week instead of sixty. She'd be able to spend a few precious hours with her baby every single day.

Baby? Chloe wouldn't be a baby much longer. Tomorrow was her first birthday. She could hardly believe it. In Lucy's constant struggle to pay rent and medical bills and child care, she'd missed much of her daughter's first year. She'd missed the first time her baby had rolled over, the first time she'd sat up by herself, the first time she'd crawled. She'd missed countless smiles and crying and happy jabbering…

Stop it, she ordered herself, angry at how close she was to tears. *Stop it right now.*

Darryl burst through the door with a hard ring of the bell, bringing a blast of wind and snow behind him.

"Hey, Luce," Darryl said with a leer on his pink, rubbery lips. "Happy New Year."

"Happy New Year," she mumbled, hating that he called her *Luce*. It reminded her of the last man who'd called her that.

"Busy tonight?"

"Yes, very," she lied over the lump in her throat.

"Let me see." She tried to flinch away, but he still managed to brush against her backside as he went behind the counter. He punched a few buttons on the cash register, then seeing the few dollars inside the tray, looked up at her accusingly. "Why, you little tease."

Pretending to laugh, she backed from him. "It's been busy, really! See the floors wet with tracked snow? I'd better get a mop…"

"Always such a busy little bee." He sneered, stopping her with one bony, sinewy hand. "You really think you're better than me, don't you?"

"No, of course not, I—"

Darryl grabbed her blue smock, looking down at her, breathing hard. "I'm tired of being nice to you for nothing."

She heard the bell jingle above the door. But before she could look, he grabbed the back of her head, coming at her with his pink, rubbery lips.

"What are you doing—let me go!"

"You act so prim," he panted, "but you sleep around. You had that kid, didn't you? I know you want me—"

"No," she whimpered, struggling to turn her face away.

Darryl yelped as a large hand grabbed him by the shoulder, spinning him around, yanking him backward like a dog on a leash.

Lucy gave a little cry as she saw a dark, towering

figure pick up her manager by the lapels of his jacket. Darryl struggled futilely while the man, far taller and stronger than him, lifted him off the floor.

The stranger's eyes were hard and black. In a voice as cold and implacable as death, he growled into his face, "Get. Out."

"Yes," Darryl gasped.

The giant tossed him to the floor. Her manager scrabbled back like a crab, tripping over his own feet in his eagerness to get away. He paused at the door.

"You're fired!" he bleated at Lucy, then rushed out into the snowy night, revving the engine of his old gray sedan down the dark street.

Fired? She was *fired*? Her heart pounding, Lucy looked at her rescuer beneath the fluorescent overhead light.

The dark stranger looked down at her. His expressive eyes seared hers. He didn't touch her. He didn't have to. Just the heat of his glance made her tremble from deep within, as if he'd just woken something deep inside her...

"Are you hurt, *signorina*?" His voice was accented and deep.

She had to lean back to see his face. She was five-six, not terribly petite, but the man still towered over her. His shoulders were impossibly broad, the lines of his long, black coat elegant and sharp, and his face...his face! Roman nose, high cheekbones. His blue eyes stood out against his olive skin. He had black, wavy hair, a darkly shadowed chin and crinkles at the edge of his eyes. Early thirties?

But he took her breath away. The way he'd saved her—the way he looked at her now. She'd never known a man could be at once so beautiful and so strong. He was like a handsome prince out of a long-forgotten dream.

"*Signorina?*" His eyes were intense, searching as he reached over to touch her cheek. "If he hurt you—"

She felt his brief touch like an explosion up and down her body. Her blood trembled as if she'd just thrown herself naked into a bed of snow. "No. I'm fine…I'm…" She sucked in her breath and repeated numbly, "I'm fired."

Fired.

No way to pay Mrs. Plotzky.

With no babysitter, she couldn't go to her two part-time jobs. And since Chloe's trip to the E.R. last month for croup, Lucy was already a month behind on her rent. Her landlord had threatened to throw her out on the street if she didn't catch up.

Cold days stretched before her, Chicago's icy wind wailing like a baby's cry, and frigid, desperate nights scavenging beds at homeless shelters. She'd be destitute with her baby in the dead of winter, no job, no money, no home…

Her baby. She'd failed her baby.

Lucy's heart rose up in her throat, nearly choking her. Her lips soundlessly repeated her daughter's name. Her knees trembled, her body shaking with a whole year of repressed grief and exhaustion. And everything started to go black…

The man caught her before she could hit the floor.

Lifting her as if she weighed nothing, he held her against his chest.

"You're done here," he growled, and started carrying her toward the door.

Carrying her to the door?

She blinked up at him, feeling dazed and light-headed—and not just because of nearly fainting. Being close to this stranger, being cradled in his arms, did strange things to her heart rate. He was as darkly handsome as any hero from a novel. As he carried her past the counter, her eyes fell upon her battered paperback copy of *Wuthering Heights* poking out of her bag on the floor.

But this dark, handsome stranger wasn't Heathcliff. And she certainly wasn't pampered, spoiled Cathy. Romantic tales had nothing to do with real life.

She'd learned that the hard way.

Lucy shook herself out of her reverie. "Where—where are you taking me?"

"Out of here."

"Put me down!" Every insane man in Chicago seemed to be stopping by tonight—all of them intent on ruining her life! She kicked and struggled in his arms. "Let me *go!*"

Abruptly he released her, and she slid down his impossibly hard, impeccably dressed body. Her own body broke out in a cold sweat as she stood somewhat shakily on her own two feet.

"I think the phrase you're looking for," the man said, "is *thank you.*"

She'd been grateful to the man for saving her from Darryl's advance, but now... What did Lucy care about some forced kiss, when her baby might soon have no home?

"Thank you?" she demanded furiously. "For what? For getting me *fired*? I could have handled Darryl just fine if you hadn't interfered!"

"*Sì.*" His sensual mouth curved upward. "You obviously had the situation well in hand."

She ground her jaw. "You're going to call him right now and tell him you're sorry!"

"I am sorry only that I didn't use his face to mop your dirty floor."

If she didn't get her job back, she would be forced to take her baby to a homeless shelter. If all the shelters were full, which was likely during Chicago's cold, hard winter, they'd have to live out of Lucy's decrepit old hatchback, on the street, freezing…

And it was all her fault for not doing a better job at protecting her daughter.

Terror ripped through her. "I need this job!"

"No. You do not." He looked down at her, so handsome, with the calm arrogance that only came from wealth. "You cannot pretend you took this job out of anything but desperation."

Lucy felt sick at his accurate appraisal of her situation. With no savings and few marketable skills, Lucy had worked at low-paying jobs since Chloe's father had deserted them a week before her birth. She'd had to work constantly just to survive, since she'd foolishly given up her hard-won college scholarship to be with him. And he'd left Lucy with nothing but his baby in her belly and the memory of his whispered promises.

For the past year, she'd held their heads above water by such a thin margin. One mistake like this could suck them under. She couldn't let them drown!

"Please," she whispered, though she knew it was hopeless. "You don't know what will happen if I lose this job."

He looked down at her. Reaching out a broad, strong-fingered hand, he gently lifted her chin.

"You have nothing to fear ever again. You are mine now, Lucia. And I protect what is mine."

She was his? What was he talking about?

Then she realized what he'd called her: *Lucia*.

"How—how did you know my name?" Lucy stammered.

"I know more about you than you can imagine." He watched her beneath heavy-lidded eyes. "And I'm here to make your dreams come true."

Her dreams.

A snug, warm little house surrounded by sunshine and flowers. Her daughter growing up happy and secure. Having someone to love, instead of always being alone, fighting just to survive—

Pulling away from his touch, she angrily shook the images from her mind.

"My only dream is for you to call Darryl and beg for forgiveness."

His dark eyebrows rose. "That is indeed a fantasy."

"What did you think I would say? That my dream was to spend a night in your bed, having you make love to me for hours on end?"

She'd meant to be sarcastic, but he gave her a hot

glance that made her shiver, and wonder if her words were truer than she'd thought.

"I offer you revenge," he said. "Against the man who hurt you."

"I told you. Darryl didn't do anything. You came before—"

"Alexander Wentworth," he bit out.

At the name, she felt the blood drain from her face. "What?"

"I will make him regret the day he abandoned you and your child to starve." His blue eyes burned through her. "You are going to come with me to Italy, and live in luxury for the rest of your life."

CHAPTER TWO

HE WANTED to take her to Italy?

Italy. The warm, beautiful land Lucy had dreamed of since she was twelve years old, watching *A Room with a View* on TV during her mother's last night in the hospital. Even her mom's final words to her had been, "Go to Italy, Lucy... Go..."

But Lucy had never left Illinois. She'd lived in foster homes until she was eighteen, then worked and scrimped her way into college. Her sophomore year, working at a department store, she'd met a handsome, smooth-talking man who spoke Italian—the vice president of a fashion house based out of New York. He delighted her with stories of Rome, promising to someday take her to visit.

Lucy had never met a man like Alex Wentworth. A man so magical...so glamorous...so exotic. She'd dropped out of college, giving up all her hard work, simply because he'd complained that school took too much of her time. She'd fallen like a brick.

She was still falling. The dream had become a nightmare. He'd fled to Rome, beyond the reach of Chicago's child support laws. For the last year, he'd returned all her letters and photographs unopened. He'd sent her one curt note, telling her he was in love with someone else. He'd suggested Chloe was not his child and that Lucy was either a delusional stalker or a gold-digging whore.

It had nearly killed her. But she was fine now. Really. She could live with a broken heart.

What she couldn't understand was how he could deny their child. How he could live in luxury, drinking wine, taking lovers, enjoying a warm, beautiful city— when he'd left his innocent baby behind to suffer?

If Lucy went to Italy, she could ask him.

Looking up at the dark stranger, she licked her dry lips. "Let me get this straight. You...you want to take me to Italy?"

He gave her a sensual smile. "*Sì*. And you will never worry about money again."

She almost couldn't breathe. The man hadn't been lying—it really *was* an offer straight out of her wildest dreams. To never have to scrimp again, wake up in a terrified panic in the middle of the night, wondering how she'd pay her bills. To know Chloe was safe and warm and secure forever.

And she could see Alex. He'd been able to ignore her letters, but he couldn't ignore her if she showed up at his office, could he? Once she showed him a picture of Chloe, he would come to his senses. He would love their beautiful baby. Once he saw their daughter, once she was real to him, how could he do anything but love her?

Lucy accepted that he'd moved on to another woman. But she couldn't bear for Chloe to grow up without a father, as she herself had. Without a father, Lucy'd had no one to love or protect her when her mother had died...

"So you agree?" the dark stranger said coolly.

Lucy clasped her hands behind her back to hide their trembling. "I don't understand. Why do you want to take me to Italy? How would that hurt Alex?"

The man gave a cold smile. "He will realize how great a fool he was to let you go."

A laugh rose in her throat, so bitter it nearly choked her. "How so?"

"He will lose something he wants. Something that rightfully belongs to me." The man reached forward, touching her shoulder. His latent power and sensuality burned through her blue cashier's smock, sending a current of heat pouring through her veins like lava. "We will make him pay, Lucia." His intense eyes mesmerized her. "All you have to do is say yes."

Yes, she thought, dazed at her own sudden change of fortune. *Yes, yes, yes.*

But as her lips parted to speak the words, a realization made her freeze.

She'd been through this before.

Attracted to a devastatingly handsome man who made her blood race. Who'd promised her the world. She'd naively given him her heart, her future, her faith.

And it had cost her everything.

She wrenched her shoulder away.

"Sorry," she forced herself to say. "I'm not interested."

He blinked.

"You're—*not interested*?"

She got the impression that no woman had ever turned him down for anything. It would have been amusing, if the whole situation hadn't infuriated her—and made her hurt all over.

Fighting back tears, she picked up her ratty handbag from the floor. "You walk in here, a total stranger. You get me fired—then expect me to blindly trust you? Are you out of your mind? Who do you think you are?"

He gave her a brief bow, elegant and fluid and ironic. The sharp cut of his coat, his blue eyes against tanned skin, reminded her of Mediterranean sun and olive groves. He was a romantic fantasy, every dream she'd ever had of exotic lands. And then he spoke.

"I am Prince Maximo d'Aquilla."

She stared at him for a shocked moment, thinking she'd heard him wrong, that she was having a flashback to all the historical novels she'd read as a teenager. "You're a prince?"

"Does my title impress you?" He punched numbers on his cell phone, the expression on his face hard as granite as he snapped it shut. "*Va bene*. Perhaps now you'll cease your pointless resistance and accept your fate."

Prince Maximo d'Aquilla. An exotic name. But he was more than a dream. He was a flesh-and-blood man, a Roman gladiator hard of sinew and bone, with a powerful, dangerous edge.

And he was too good to be true.

She shook her head. "I'm not going anywhere with you."

"I grow weary of this." His eyes traced over her. "I do not have time. We both know you're coming with me. Either do it gracefully, or—" he came closer "—I will simply take you."

She could see at once that it was not an idle threat. He could take her—in any way he wished. And on this dark, empty, snowy night, with no cameras or weapons or customers, who would stop him?

She sucked in her breath, gathering her anger like a defensive force. *She* would stop him.

How dare he try to intimidate her this way! Did he think he could boss her around with his gorgeous face, his wealth, his power, his alleged *royalty*?

"Do you think I'm stupid?" she demanded.

"I'm starting to wonder."

"Your story is ridiculous! You're a prince, and you want me to run away with you to Italy and be rich and happy? What's your scam? I get on your plane, then what—end up sold into a harem in some desert?"

"You think any sheikh would tolerate such insolence?" he said icily.

"I just know that when a handsome man makes an offer that's too good to be true, it means *he's lying*."

His laser-blue eyes narrowed.

"First you insult my honor. Now you call me a liar?"

His voice held a quiet, dangerous edge. She trembled with fear, even as she rebelliously clenched her hands.

"If you think I'm idiotic enough to believe some fantasy about becoming wealthy and getting revenge on Alex, you're not just a liar, you're a fool."

He looked down at her, and she felt scorching heat

to her toes. His glance made her feel hot all over, dizzy, pummeled by a whirlwind. "If you were a man, I would make you regret those insults."

She raised her chin defiantly. "And since I'm a woman?"

His fingers gently traced a tendril of dark hair that had escaped her ponytail. "Your punishment will be entirely different."

There was a sudden ring at the door. It took a moment for Lucy to even realize what that meant, lost as she was in the sensation tingling up her hair, her scalp, down her spine to her toes. How was it possible that with just a single touch, he could make her whole body shake…?

A hulking man, shorter than Maximo but twice as wide, came to him with a deferential bow. *"Mio principe."*

"Ermanno." The two men spoke in Italian, one giving calm commands, the other acquiescing with a nod.

For a moment, she stared at Maximo. A gorgeous, wealthy, arrogant prince. Demanding that she go with him to Italy. *Her*, Lucy Abbott. A nobody.

No! she told herself fiercely. She wasn't a nobody. She was Chloe's mother. And she couldn't succumb to this so-called prince's evil scheme, whatever it might be. She wouldn't obey. And the fact that his slightest caress made her ache to surrender only proved how dangerous he truly was.

Now. While he was distracted—this was her chance to escape. Before he dragged her away to hell under the guise of sweet promises, and she never saw her daughter again.

Quietly she edged back toward the door.

The two men continued to talk.

Lucy took a deep breath. Then turned and ran.

"Ferma!" the dark prince roared. "Stop, Lucia!"

Outside, the blast of cold air hit her, swirling snow and making her long dark ponytail twist in the wind. Pushing up her glasses, she sprinted for her old Honda. Parked behind the gas station, it was covered by ice and snow. Her hand shook as she stuck the key in the door.

But the lock was frozen!

Panicking, she glanced over her shoulder.

Prince Maximo was striding toward her like a bull, his dark eyes cold and furious. Desperate, she turned it harder.

The key broke off in her hand.

She had no car. *No escape.*

With a gasp, she turned and stumbled through the snow, crossing the street toward the deserted city park. On the other side of the vast, empty darkness she could see lights and the twinkle of traffic. But she'd barely reached the edge of the park before he caught up with her.

He knocked her into the soft powder, his large, muscled body pressing her into the snow. Grabbing her wrists, he turned her over beneath him. She struggled, but he used his weight against her.

She looked up at his face, so close to hers. With his body so hard and warm against her own, she could barely feel the cold snow beneath her.

"Basta! I told you to stop!" He tightened his hands, shackling her wrists. "You must learn to obey."

The trees were dark over his head, their snowy branches waving like claws against the gray sky. Scattered moonlight sifted through the clouds, leaving his dark hair in a halo of light.

"I'll never obey you," she cried. "Never!"

"We'll see." His glance touched her lips, and she suddenly knew he was going to kiss her. In the dark winter wonderland of the park, they were utterly alone. Surrounded by snow and cold, she felt fire in her veins at his touch, and she was helpless to move, helpless to fight.

But she had to fight. Without a mother to protect her, her baby would be vulnerable and alone, tossed into foster care as Lucy herself once had been. She couldn't give in.

She would fight to protect Chloe to her last breath…

"Let me go," she whispered. "Please. If you have any decency at all—if you've ever loved anyone and lost them—I'm begging you. Let me go."

Her quiet voice reverberated against the snow, muffled in the thick silence of the night.

He stared down at her with sudden pain in his eyes.

Abruptly he released her wrists and rose to his feet.

"As you wish, *cara mia*," he said, sounding almost bored. "Stay here if you wish. I am returning to my hotel."

Thank you, thank you, thank you, she thought fervently. She scrambled to her feet, turning on her heel, ready to run.

"After all," he mused behind her, "I want to make sure your baby is sleeping comfortably. And she hasn't lost that little purple hippo she carries everywhere."

Her heart stopped in her chest.

Wide-eyed with fear, she whirled back to face him. "What?"

He looked at her with cool disdain. "Oh, did I not tell you? My men picked up your daughter an hour ago."

CHAPTER THREE

"YOU aren't going to get away with this," Lucy ground out for the tenth time as he drove them into downtown Chicago.

Unmoved, Maximo parked his sleek black Mercedes beneath the grand marquee of the Drake Hotel. "You have no idea what I can get away with."

Furious, she ripped off her blue cashier's smock, balling it up in her hands and tossing it to the floor. "I don't know what the laws are like in Italy, but in Chicago, you can't just *kidnap* someone—"

"There are laws against kidnapping in Italy, as well." He abruptly stopped the car. "They do not apply in this case. I did not kidnap your daughter."

"What do you call it then?"

"I knew you would accept my offer. I simply expedited our departure."

Leaving the engine idling, he undid his seat belt and stepped out of the black SUV. Her eyes widened as she saw him carelessly hand a hundred-dollar bill to the waiting valet.

"Thank you, your highness," the young man breathed, and hurried to open the passenger-side door for Lucy. She nearly tripped over her own feet running after Maximo. With his long stride, he was already to the main door.

"Welcome back, your highness." The brawny doorman touched his cap with deep respect. "Happy New Year to you, sir."

"*Grazie,*" Maximo replied with a brief smile. "To you, as well."

Just inside the revolving door, Lucy caught up with him on the wide flight of stairs leading up to the lobby. She grabbed his arm. "You have them all fooled, don't you?" she snapped. "Some *prince*. They think you're respectable—honorable—but I know the truth. You're nothing but a..."

He looked at her hand, then back up. His blue eyes were icier than Lake Michigan in winter. "I'm what?"

Fury pounded through her, making her reckless. "A thief. A blackmailer. A kidnapper of children—"

He grabbed her shoulders. She felt the strength of his touch. He looked down, towering over her. His handsome face was as cold and hard as ever; there was something new beneath his eyes—something ferocious and angry, held back by the sheerest force of will.

Looking up into his face, she was suddenly afraid.

His voice was low. "Be careful how you provoke me."

She swallowed, remembering his earlier promise to punish her like a woman deserved. "I'm not scared of you," she lied. "And if you think taking me to your hotel room—forcing me into bed—will hurt Alexander, you're dead wrong."

He abruptly released her.

"I've never forced any woman into my bed," he said coolly. His eyes traced her face, then up and down the length of her body. "If I ever decide I want you, *cara*, you'll come to me willingly."

The colossal arrogance of the man! A hot flush suffused her cheeks. "How dare you—"

"Fortunately you are not my type," he said. "You are far too plain, too badly dressed, too young—"

"Oh," she gasped, humiliated to the core.

"You are not a woman to me," he said coldly. "You are a weapon."

A weapon? She sucked in her breath. "What do you intend to do to Alex?"

"Why do you care? Unless you're still in love with him."

She shook her head. "Of course not! But he's my baby's father!"

"Don't worry." His lip curled into a sneer. "He will merely be forced to admit that he has a daughter. Surely you have no objection to that?"

Alex had been keeping Chloe a secret? "No," she muttered. "I've no objection."

"And he will lose his bid for a company. Someone else—someone you don't know—will also lose."

"How many enemies do you have, anyway?" Lucy demanded, then shook her head. "Hundreds. Thousands. Everyone who's ever met you, I imagine! I don't care. Just take me to my daughter. If you've hurt or frightened her, I swear I'll—"

"I would never hurt a child, *signorina*. Just as I would

never hurt a woman." His lip curled as he added under his breath, "Although you tempt me."

She followed him up the steps to the elegant 1920s-style lobby. The soaring ceiling sparkled with enormous chandeliers. Beneath them, wealthy revelers crowded together, some wearing diamonds and fur coats, celebrating the advent of the new year with a half-drunken chorus of "Auld Lang Syne."

Maximo led her past the well-heeled guests to the golden elevators behind the lobby. When they were alone behind the closed doors, he hit the button for the tenth floor.

Lucy repeated in a low voice, "I don't even know you. So I don't understand why you've done this. Kidnapped my daughter. Gotten me fired. Turned my life upside down—"

He turned to face her. "Don't you want to be rich, Lucia?" he demanded. "To buy clothes, cars, jewelry? Don't you wish to spend time with your daughter and buy her everything her heart desires?"

She stared at him, heart pounding in her chest. "Are you crazy? Of course I do! But strangers don't just fall out of the sky and offer money. I'm trying to figure out your angle!"

"No angle. I'm offering a lifetime of wealth and luxury for you and your daughter. And the chance to repay the man who abandoned you both."

"But there's a catch," she said.

"What makes you so sure?"

"There's always a catch."

"Perhaps." He looked at her. "Does it matter?"

The elevator doors opened, and he strode out. Feeling as if she were Alice who'd just fallen through the looking glass, Lucy followed him down the maroon carpet of the hallway. The wainscoted walls were yellow-gold, illuminated by glistening chandeliers at every corner. He stopped at a door.

Mrs. Plotzky opened to his knock. Her hair was in curlers and she was wearing a luxurious white robe and cushy hotel slippers. The television was blaring softly behind her in the elegant living room. She beamed at sight of Lucy.

"Oh my dear! Such a wonderful day! I'm so happy for you. When Prince Maximo's bodyguards explained he was taking you both to Italy, I—"

"Where's Chloe?" Lucy bit out, angry that her babysitter had been so gullible.

Taken aback, the elderly woman pointed to a door inside the suite. Mrs. Plotzky sat back down on the gold sofa with her knitting while Lucy went to the adjacent door.

She stood in the doorway of the darkened bedroom, listening to her daughter's deep, even breathing. When Lucy's eyes had adjusted, she saw a small lump in the center of the enormous bed surrounded by pillows. Her baby. The light from the doorway scattered across Chloe's plump cheeks. The baby was clutching her tattered purple hippo to her chest.

Lucy crept closer. She stroked Chloe's hair, tenderly tucking the blankets beneath her chubby legs. The linens made her pause. They were soft against Lucy's fingers. Luxurious and white, not stained and threadbare from a thousand washings at the quarter Laundromat.

Slowly she looked around the palatial bedroom. From the windows overlooking Lake Michigan, to the plush, pristine carpet, the room had every luxury and comfort.

Not like their tiny apartment, where the windows rattled every time the El train went by. Where Chloe's crib was crammed against Lucy's bed, which was jammed up against the kitchen counter. Where it was cold all winter, no matter how high Lucy turned up the thermostat. Where spiders and mice kept turning up, no matter how hard or often Lucy cleaned in the middle of the night.

Chloe turned over in her sleep, stretching in the luxurious bed with a contented sigh. Lucy's heart went to her throat.

Her baby deserved a life like *this*.

Don't you want to be rich? she heard Maximo's voice say. *Don't you wish to spend time with your daughter and buy her everything her heart desires?*

Stroking Chloe's soft downy hair, Lucy saw the worn-out elbows of her baby's pajamas, and her throat started to hurt.

Alex had told her he loved her. He'd proposed marriage. He'd begged Lucy to have his baby. He'd refused to use a condom, laughing at her fears, seducing her, reassuring her. Older than her, with a high-status job, he'd promised to give them both security and comfort and love—forever.

Against her better judgment, she'd let herself love him. Let herself *believe*.

Then she'd come home on Christmas Eve last year.

Heavily pregnant, weighed down with grocery bags of fresh cranberries and canned pumpkin, she'd been singing "Deck the Halls" when she pushed open the door with her hip. She'd found her apartment empty and dark. All his clothes were gone. His toothbrush. His briefcase. His computer. Even the three-carat engagement ring she'd left lovingly in the velvet box on her dresser, because it no longer fit her pregnancy-bloated finger.

Everything. Gone.

A year later, and Lucy still couldn't hear "Deck the Halls" on the radio without feeling sick.

He'd left her, but that didn't matter. What did matter was that he'd left his own child to starve. He'd even tried to deny Chloe was his.

Lucy would never forgive him for that.

Just as she would never forgive herself for trusting his easy charm. She could still hear his whisper sometimes at night. "I love ya, Luce. I'll always take care of you."

Liar, she thought, then looked down at her daughter. Alex had lost more than he would ever know.

But so had Chloe. She had no father.

Lucy's eyes narrowed. If she could just see Alex, she could break through his selfish stupor and he would realize what he'd done. He would realize that he loved his daughter. He would act like a decent father, and her daughter would be safe and warm, with two parents to protect her.

Lucy could still give her precious baby the life she deserved.

Whatever it took.

Whatever the catch.

To give her baby a good life, Lucy would do anything—work herself to exhaustion. Sell her body. Even risk her soul.

In sudden decision, Lucy softly kissed Chloe goodnight. She spoke briefly with Mrs. Plotzky before leaving the elderly babysitter knitting in front of her game show.

Every step Lucy took was deliberate. Determined.

She found Maximo in the gold-and-cream hallway, leaning against the wall.

"Well?" he asked quietly. "What is your decision?"

She raised her chin. "My daughter will never worry about money again? She'll have food and a warm house and be happy and safe?"

"Correct."

"And I will be able to speak with Alex in person?"

His blue eyes glittered. "Oh, yes."

"I accept your offer."

CHAPTER FOUR

"*VA BENE.*" Maximo looked down at her with a strange light in his eyes. "Come with me."

He took her hand, and she felt the same electricity, the same high-voltage shock. He pulled her back down the hallway and into the elevator. He was Heathcliff carrying her across the moors. He was Mr. Rochester demanding what he had no right to possess...

He was Prince Maximo d'Aquilla, taking her to his hotel room.

He stood behind her in the elevator, his hands possessively on her shoulders. Against her will, she closed her eyes. The weight of his hands felt like gold against her skin. Satiny-smooth, gleaming, heavy—forbidden.

Except Maximo wasn't Heathcliff. Heathcliff had wanted Cathy so much that he'd been willing to kill for her, die for her. He'd been driven half-mad when he'd lost her.

The Italian prince standing behind her now, so close that she could feel the warmth emanating from his body, didn't even see her as a woman.

You're not my type. You're too plain. Too badly dressed. Too young.

That's wonderful, she told herself fiercely. She was done with men. Done with love. All she cared about now was Chloe, and giving her a good life at any cost.

The elevator stopped on the fifth floor, and Maximo led her to the end of a hall. She heard laughter, the chiming of crystal glasses, voices speaking in English and Italian over the sounds of violins. He pushed open the door to his suite.

Lucy stopped, her mouth agape.

In the far corner, a string quartet performed Vivaldi's "Winter." She recognized two Hollywood celebrities, a senator. Money and power poured from the suite like music.

She'd expected a hotel suite, but…

"This is a palace!"

"I don't have any palaces in this particular country." Looking utterly at ease, Maximo took off his coat and tossed it on the upholstered settee beneath the mirrored foyer. "This is just the presidential suite."

Just the presidential suite. One night here would probably cost a year of her rent. "You're having a New Year's Eve party?"

He glanced at her, his eyes heavy-lidded, sensual. "I will soon celebrate far more than that. Stay here."

Glamorous people were turning to stare. Two women in particular, a blonde and a brunette, whispered to each other as they looked Lucy up and down. She licked her lips nervously. "Perhaps I should wait for you outside—"

"You will wait here." His voice rang with authority,

demanding immediate obedience. "If anyone speaks to you, you will not explain your presence."

"No problem," she muttered. How could she explain it, when even she didn't understand?

She watched him make his way toward the bar across the suite, frequently stopped by his guests. Every woman in the suite, young and old, married and single, seemed determined to get his attention.

Except for the two gorgeous, elegant women who'd seen her arrive with Maximo. They sashayed toward Lucy like vultures.

The pretty blonde in a tight red dress looked at her scornfully, and Lucy was suddenly aware of her scuffed tennis shoes, her messy ponytail, her old clothes. The blonde's lips twisted. "Nice outfit."

Lucy flushed. She knew her sweatshirt was not fashionable, but it had once been her mother's. Working the night shift, that made her feel watched over; plus, the kitten on its front always made Chloe laugh.

"I've heard of slumming," the blonde drawled, "but this is ridiculous, isn't it, Esmé?"

"Now, Arabella. You should be more kind." The chic brunette gave Lucy a patronizing stare. "She's probably here to clean the bathrooms."

Lucy froze, reminded of the way she'd been teased as a child. Her mom had moved them around so much, Lucy had always been the new kid in school. With her thick glasses and secondhand clothes, she'd been an easy target. And after her mother died, it had been worse. She'd spent countless hours in the school library with books her only real friends....

"Esmé. Arabella." Maximo suddenly appeared at Lucy's shoulder. He leaned forward to kiss the cheeks of the brunette, then the blonde. At his attention, the women preened and tossed their hair, like flowers reaching for the sun.

He drew back, putting his hand on Lucy's arm. "I see you've met Lucia."

Esmé tossed Lucy a cold glare, then pretended to give a little laugh. "Oh. Is she your friend? I thought she was the maid. How very eccentric of you, Maximo. Why go out for a common drive-through hamburger when you could enjoy foie gras in the comfort of your suite?"

She obviously wasn't talking about food.

For Lucy, it was the last straw in a stressful night.

"Foie gras is outlawed in Chicago, Esmé," Lucy replied sweetly. "I can't imagine why anyone would find mashed duck liver appealing, anyway." She looked the brunette over from her supershort minidress to her platform heels, "It's so greasy and nasty."

Her eyes narrowed. "Why, you little—"

"Excuse us," Maximo said, hiding a smile as he pressed Lucy away.

"It's almost midnight, Maximo," Esmé called after them as they reached the bedroom doorway. "Don't forget our New Year's kiss!"

"No!" the blonde cried. "He's going to kiss *me*!"

Maximo closed the door solidly behind them, and just like that, all the noise of the party fell away. They were alone in the bedroom.

Lucy rubbed her wrist.

"I'm sorry," she muttered, although she really wasn't.

"Sorry? For what?"

"For being rude to your mistress."

He stared at her, then snorted. "Do you mean Lady Arabella? Or the Countess of Bedingford?"

Lady? Countess? Apparently royal titles were as common in Maximo's world as Mr. or Mrs. "Take your pick."

He shrugged. "I hardly think a meaningless fling qualifies any woman to claim the title of *mistress*."

"Meaning you've slept with both of them?" Her shocked voice ended with a squeak.

His sensual mouth curved into a smile. "There have been many women in my life. But as for details—a gentleman can hardly be expected to kiss and tell."

"Some gentleman," she huffed. "Can't you tell that they're in love with you?"

"I doubt that very much."

"They were ready to scratch my eyes out just for being with you!"

"You exaggerate. And in any case—" his blue eyes caressed hers "—if any woman chooses to love me, she has only herself to blame. I am always very clear. I am not a man to settle down or give my heart to just one woman. I am faithful to only three things."

"Those are?" she spat out, folding her arms.

"Justice for my family. My own freedom." He held out a crystal flute of champagne. "And the success of my company."

She stared at the champagne he was holding out to her. As a college student, she'd been too focused on her studies to bother with alcohol; as a single mother, she hadn't had the money or inclination. "Look, I know it's New Year's and everything, but I'm just not in the mood. If you want to celebrate, why don't you ask one of the princesses outside?"

His dark eyebrow lifted in amusement. "Surely you're not jealous?"

She looked away. "I just feel sorry for them, that's all."

"Esmé and Arabella have influence in certain circles, and though I've lost personal interest I see no reason to cut off ties with them. I trade in luxury. And that is what I celebrate. The takeover of a small leather-goods company for my conglomerate. I have desired this company for many years," he said softly. "And it will be mine within the hour. Perhaps you've heard of it. Ferrazzi."

He watched her from beneath heavily-lidded eyes.

Ferrazzi. She'd admired their three-thousand-dollar handbags, even sold a few of them to wealthy customers. They were lovely bags, impossibly stylish, with leather as soft as cashmere and hardy as steel.

But worth that price? The bags weren't big enough to live in, nor did they magically mop her floor, cook her dinner or wash her clothes. Three thousand dollars for a handbag? That was insane!

But Maximo seemed to be waiting for a response, and it seemed rude to criticize the company he would soon own. She cleared her throat, struggling to be polite. "Ferrazzi. Yes."

His large hand tightened around his delicate champagne flute. "What do you know about it?"

"Um." She bit her lip—literally—then finally said with a sigh, "I once worked in the accessories department at Neiman Marcus. Of course I know Ferrazzi handbags. That's like asking me if I've ever heard of Chanel or Prada. You're buying the company?"

"*Sì.*"

"But it must cost millions!"

He gave her a cold smile. "Hundreds of millions."

She gaped at him, then snapped her mouth closed, muttering, "You obviously have more money than sense."

"And you obviously have greater regard for truth than tact. Here." At a discreet knock on the door, he pushed the flute into her hand. Swiftly downing his own champagne, Maximo answered the door. A slender man in a suit handed him a folder.

"What is it?" she asked, taking a tentative sip of champagne. *Not bad*, she thought in surprise. It was a bit sweet and fizzy like soda.

Closing the door behind him, Maximo opened the folder and glanced over the papers. He handed her the folder. "This if for you to sign."

Setting the champagne flute down on a glass table, she opened it with a puzzled frown. "What is it?"

"A prenuptial agreement."

"But—who's getting married?"

"You are. To me."

CHAPTER FIVE

LUCY looked up from the folder to the handsome prince in front of her. "What are you talking about?" she croaked. "Married? To you?"

"Correct."

"I don't even know you!"

His sensual lips curved. "An excellent start for marriage."

"You said you'd never settle down with one woman—and you want to marry me?"

"*Sì.*"

"But why?"

"Let's start with why you'd want to marry me," he said smoothly. "My palatial homes all over the world. My vast fortune. You can buy whatever you want without question. You will never need to work again. You will travel in the most exclusive circles of society. Your daughter will go to the best schools." He took a step toward her. "And then there's the title."

"The title?" she repeated faintly, aware of how close he was to her.

He stroked a dark tendril of her hair, still wet from when he'd crushed her into the snow. "Wherever you go, for the rest of your life, you will be accepted and admired. As my princess. My bride," he said. "The Principessa Lucia d'Aquilla."

Lucy—a *princess*?

Suddenly alcohol seemed like a terrific idea. Snatching up her champagne flute, she drank it all down in a gulp. The expensive bubbles might really have been soda for all she noticed. But when she was finished, her mouth was still dry. She licked her lips, then felt his searing blue gaze. She looked up.

His hot glance plundered her mouth. As if he'd seized her, kissed her, possessed her by force of his will. She was suddenly aware of her every breath—and his.

"But people don't get married for *money*," she whispered. "They do it because they care about each other…"

"Oh, do they?" He ran his hands on her shoulders, tracing upward with a finger along her neck to her jawline. He gently lifted her chin. He looked at her slowly, as if assessing the shape of her face beneath her glasses and messy hair, analyzing the shape of her body beneath her clothes. Finally he met her eyes.

"Perhaps you are right," he said abruptly. "Perhaps this will be for more than money. Perhaps I will take you to my bed."

"You what?"

He smiled, a cruelly sensual smile. "This will be even more enjoyable than I thought. I will make you feel as you've never felt before. Make you moan and gasp with pleasure until you forget your own name."

She closed her eyes. She knew he could do it. Just hearing him threaten to seduce her, feeling his touch against her skin, was nearly enough to make her forget her name already.

"Would you like that?" His lips brushed against the tender flesh of her ear. "Would you like, at last, to feel the sensations you've only read about in books?"

A quiet shiver rocked her from her toes.

Startled, she looked up at him. His expression was arrogant. Knowing. As if he could read into her very soul. As if he somehow knew that her only lover had left her deeply unsatisfied.

"But you said—you said you didn't want me," she stammered. "You said I'm not your type."

"I see now that I was wrong." He gently stroked down her neck with his forefinger and his thumb. "You have your own beauty, different from any I've seen before. There is no reason not to enjoy our short marriage. I can show you what love is truly like—show you how passionate love can be."

Her heart turned over. "Love?"

"Marry me, and your feet will barely touch the ground."

Oh. That kind of love. Of course, what else could he mean? A playboy like Prince Maximo d'Aquilla would not get emotionally entangled in relationships. He had too many of them.

"But you said you'd never settle down," she whispered. "So why now, Maximo? Why me?"

"You think little of yourself." He ran his hands down her arms, from her neck to her bare wrists. "You do not know your own worth, Lucia."

Lucia. Every time he called her that it was a caress, making her feel exotic, beautiful, desired. She loved the feeling—almost as much as she feared it...

She took a deep breath.

If a handsome man seems too good to be true, she repeated to herself fiercely, he's *lying.*

So why was he trying to make her believe he desired her?

Because he thought she'd refused his proposal.

The realization gave her the strength to pull away. Narrowing her eyes, she raised her chin.

"You're not proposing marriage because you think I'm *beautiful,*" she said evenly. She held up the prenup with a loud rattle of paper. "You had your lawyers working on this for hours. Stop trying to seduce me. I'm not one of those simpering women to melt at your command. Tell me *why* you want to marry me. Whom will it hurt? And how?"

"Cara—" He moved toward her, palms up in a gesture of supplication.

"No!" She moved backward, unwilling to let him touch her. "Don't you *'cara'* me. I want cold, hard facts!"

His expression changed.

And suddenly, he laughed aloud.

"Bravo, signorina," he said with a satisfied clap of his hands. "You are the first woman to resist me since I was fifteen years old. Bravo." He gave her a nod. "I respect your intelligence."

She flushed, feeling unaccountably pleased by his praise.

"And as you've left me no choice..." He took the file

from her, opening it on a nearby table. "Here are your *cold, hard facts*. Our marriage will last approximately three months. I will allow you to spend my fortune as if it were your own. In return, I will have complete control and management of all your current and future assets." He paused, looking up to search her gaze. "Do you find that unfair?"

She said with a bitter laugh, "My only asset is a beat-up old Honda that barely runs. If you want to try to manage that, be my guest."

"At the end of our marriage, I will be required to pay you full market value for anything I keep." He quickly turned to another page. "And in addition, I will recompense you with a settlement of ten million dollars for each month of our marriage."

She stared at him, unable to comprehend the words.

"Thirty...million...dollars?" she choked.

"*Sì.*"

Lucy closed her eyes. She would never have to work again. She could spend her days playing with her baby. Chloe would have the best of everything. The best schools. Brand-new toys. Brand-new clothes. Ballet lessons. Italian lessons. Tuba lessons. Anything and everything. They could have the snug, warm little house she'd always dreamed of. She could turn the heat up as high as she wished. They could pick the biggest Christmas tree on the lot. Chloe could have pony rides—no, a whole stable of thoroughbreds. World cruises. Tuition to Harvard. *Anything and everything.*

She tried to be calm, but her hands were shaking.

"Wh-what would you expect me to do for that?"

"I would expect you to appear to be my devoted wife in every way. To honor and obey."

She licked her dry lips. "To do something illegal?"

"No."

"Immoral?"

"That is in the eye of the beholder. It would be a marriage of convenience. A few moments ago, you found that distasteful. Do you still?"

She was suddenly willing to reconsider. "Just three months?"

"That is my guess." His blue eyes became grim. "I'm waiting for a man to die—a man you don't know."

That brought her up short. "Oh."

"He is old and ill. Once he is dead, we will divorce. And you will be wealthier than your wildest dreams."

"Still." She swallowed. "It's a bit ghoulish, isn't it—waiting for someone to die?"

"We all die sometime, *cara*."

"That's…true." Biting her lip, she paced the bedroom, then turned with a sudden intake of breath. "You will do nothing to cause his death?"

His eyes flashed. "You think I'm a murderer?"

She didn't know what to think. None of this made sense. "I'm just trying to understand."

"Don't try." He pushed the prenup toward her. "Just sign."

"Wait. Please." She pressed her fingers against her eyelids. *Think*, she ordered her brain. But everything he'd said, all his seductive evasions and cryptic demands, just jumbled together in her mind. Why would a wealthy, handsome prince want to marry her?

"What about me is so special that it's worth thirty million dollars?" she asked. "And what does Alex have to do with it?"

He looked away, clenching his jaw. When he turned back to her, his sky-blue gaze was cold.

"I've made you a good offer. If you don't like it, tell me to go to hell. Go back to your old life."

A sudden rush of fear went through her. Go back to her old life? Wake Chloe up from her soft bed upstairs, and drag her back to their freezing, mouse-infested apartment?

"Or—" he pushed the prenuptial agreement toward her on the table, holding out a pen "—sign this and marry me."

"But—"

"No more discussion. Make your choice."

She stared at his outstretched pen.

She'd be a fool to sign this agreement. Without a lawyer to explain the legal jargon, for all she knew she'd be signing her life away. Marry a man she didn't know? Run away with this darkly handsome prince to Italy? Be transformed from a desperate single mother to a powerful princess? Be so wealthy that her daughter, her granddaughter and her great-granddaughter would all be able to devote their lives to their own pursuit of happiness?

Slowly Lucy took the pen.

She'd be a fool *not* to sign it.

Her choice was simple. Either take this risk—or take Chloe back to their old life. One paycheck away from living out of Lucy's car. And she'd just lost her job!

Thirty million dollars. A number beyond comprehension. But still, she hesitated.

"What about your needs?"

"My needs?"

"Your—needs," she said, flushing. "I won't share your bed."

"Ah." His sensual lips slid into a grin. "We'll see."

"No." She gripped the pen in her hand. "I'd be a fool to love a man like you."

"We're not talking of love. I've taken many women to my bed, and never once experienced a broken heart. Just pleasure."

Which was exactly why she had to make sure he never touched her. A playboy prince like Maximo might be able to seduce someone with just his body, but Lucy didn't think she could keep her heart out of it. She didn't think she could make love without *falling* in love.

And one broken heart had been enough. She had to protect herself for Chloe's sake. She wanted to be a joyful, loving mother, not a depressed, empty shell of a woman.

"I don't care what you seem to think." Lucy raised her chin. "I won't be forced into your bed."

"Do you really think I would have to force you, *cara?*" He softly stroked her lips with his fingertip. She felt the masculine roughness of his skin against her tender mouth. Explosions of desire blossomed up and down her body like flowers.

He smiled down at her.

"If I choose to seduce you, you will be mine."

Yes, she thought, staring up at him in a daze.

With a sudden, harsh intake of breath, she wrenched her head away.

"I will not be yours," she bit out. "Ever."

"A challenge. How delicious." He stroked her cheek. "You are full of surprises."

Her whole body ached for him to kiss her. But she had to resist. *Resist*, she ordered her unresponsive limbs. But she couldn't move as he lowered his head toward her.

Then a knock sounded at the bedroom door.

"This is your last chance." Maximo looked down at her, cupping her chin. "Sign the agreement. Or go back to your old life. At the stroke of midnight, my offer ends."

It was nearly midnight now! Lucy glanced at the clock, then took a deep breath. Gripping the pen in her hand, she did what she knew she had to do.

She bent over the desk.

She hesitated.

Then she signed her name.

The instant she'd finished her signature, Maximo took the pen from her fingers. His expression was inscrutable. *"Bene."*

She felt dirty—as if she'd just sold her soul to the devil. And for all she knew, she had.

For you, my baby, she whispered soundlessly. *Whatever happens to me, you'll be safe.*

Maximo opened the door. Two men entered the bedroom. "This is my lawyer, Stanford Walsh, and Judge Darlington, who will marry us."

"Right now?"

"Sì." Maximo popped his head out of the door. "Esmé, Arabella—come here, *per favore.*"

"Yes, Maximo?" the countess purred.

"What do you need, your highness?" the blonde cooed.

Maximo gave them his most charming smile. "Witnesses for my wedding."

CHAPTER SIX

THE day Lucy had discovered she was pregnant, she'd started planning her dream wedding. A little white church in springtime. Flowers in bloom. A fluffy white dress. A homemade cake with white buttercream frosting. Alex next to her. And in her arms, the honorary flower girl or ring bearer—their baby.

Lucy had never imagined she would marry a stranger in a hotel, with no church, no cake and no dress. When she'd gotten ready for work that afternoon, wearing jeans, her mother's old sweatshirt, a ponytail and no makeup—she'd never imagined she was getting dressed for her *wedding*.

She had no friends. No family. The only witnesses were Maximo's thin-faced lawyer and the two gorgeous women glaring bullets into Lucy's back.

Strangely Lucy had no difficulty promising to love, honor and obey Maximo. It was almost pathetically easy. She repeated the judge's words, echoing Maximo's responses, hypnotized by his gaze. His eyes pinned her, searing her, controlling her will. Burning into her with the intensity of pure blue flame.

He slipped a gold band on her finger, and just like that, it was over.

"You'll file the license?" Maximo said quietly, shaking the judge's hand.

"It will all be arranged. As of this moment, you are married." The judge beamed at her. "Congratulations. Best wishes to you both."

"Such a beautiful ceremony." The blonde sniffled. Lucy turned in surprise to see her dabbing her mascara with a tissue. "So romantic."

But Esmé, the brunette, was staring at Lucy in shock.

"How did you do it?" she whispered. "You're nothing. Just look at you." She slowly looked Lucy up and down. "For three years, I've been starving myself to be thin. Exercising till I dropped. Spending a fortune on clothes. Following him around the world in hopes of one glance, one kiss." Her beautifully made-up face was numb. "How did you do it? *How did you make him love you?*"

Lucy sucked in her breath. Half an hour ago, she'd despised the countess. Now she felt desperately sorry for her. The woman was in love with a man who didn't deserve it—a playboy who was incapable of love.

Lucy wanted to comfort her, to explain, *He doesn't love me.* "Countess—"

But Maximo grabbed her wrist, glowering down at her as if he knew what she'd been about to say.

"Come with me, my bride."

He pulled her out of the bedroom, and into the party being celebrated in his presidential suite. The loud honking of noisemakers reverberated over cheering in Italian and English.

"The world must believe we are in love," he ground out in a low voice. "You will tell no one of our arrangement."

"But she's in love with you!"

The clinking of crystal glasses intensified as everyone rushed to refill their glasses with champagne.

"You swore to honor and obey. And yet you again attempt to defy me."

The party guests crowding the rooms of the lavish suite started a drunken countdown to the brand-new year.

"Ten…"

He pulled her close, his intent clear in his smoldering blue eyes. "And now you will pay."

"Nine…"

As if they were the only two people in the room, Maximo held her in his strong arms.

"Eight…"

"No," she gasped, trembling at the sensation of his hard body against her own. "Please——"

"Seven…"

Over the raucous noise of the party, he spoke directly into her ear, pressing his rough, scratchy cheek against her own. "You've challenged me."

"Six…"

A group of young men started cheering noisily in Italian.

"Intrigued me."

"Five…"

An elderly couple toasted each other, smiling tenderly.

Lucy looked up into her husband's handsome face. "But I don't—don't want—"

"Four…"

Maximo stroked her cheek, tilting up her head as, with agonizing slowness, he lowered his mouth near hers. "What don't you want?"

"Three…"

Her lips were full, swollen beneath his gaze. Her breasts were taut, her nipples hard and aching for his touch.

"A kiss," she whispered.

"Two…"

Saying *a kiss* caused her lips to brush against his. Her mouth sizzled, sending waves of longing from the tip of her tongue to the sudden ache between her legs.

Desire for him arched her body like an electric current—desire she was fighting with all her might. She couldn't let him kiss her. She couldn't let him start their marriage off that way. If she did, who knew where it would end?

"One! Happy New Year!"

The whole suite went crazy, embracing each other and tossing party hats in the air. The string quartet burst into a rendition of "Auld Lang Syne."

And her dark prince kissed her.

His lips were featherlight. She tried to push him away, battering at his shoulders, but as his kiss became more passionate, more ardent, she sagged in his arms. He drew her closer. His large hands wrapped around her hips, holding her firmly against his body. There was no space between them as his tongue flicked against her mouth, spreading her lips, entwining her in a sensual caress.

His kiss shot through her, pulsing a burst of light down her veins, exploding from her fingertips and toes.

A blast of desire crashed through her like lightning splitting the sky.

She forgot the guests around them—the senators and starlets.

Forgot the thirty million dollars.

Forgot she'd vowed never to give herself to another man.

She knew only that this was meant to be. *She was meant to be his woman...*

An eternity—or a second—later, he drew away from her. And he looked down into her star-filled eyes.

"*Sì, cara, sì,*" he whispered, stroking her cheek. "You'll be mine."

His at last.

As his Gulfstream IV jet began the descent into Milan, Maximo closed his laptop and looked at his new bride. She was sleeping on the white leather sofa across from his, cuddling her slumbering baby in her arms.

Lucia Ferrazzi. *Per miracolo*, he'd found her. And with the prenuptial agreement, he'd made sure that she and her daughter would be protected and safe forever. He'd never need to feel guilty again. He'd be free.

And his revenge on her grandfather was at hand. For the rest of the old man's life—however short it might be—he would know that he'd lost everything to Maximo. His precious company. His granddaughter. Giuseppe Ferrazzi would believe that Lucia loved her husband. He would see her and she would be completely under Maximo's control.

The old man would hear that his granddaughter and

great-granddaughter had been found, but he would never be allowed to speak to either of them. Giuseppe Ferrazzi would die penniless. Alone. Just as he deserved.

Maximo's lips curved into a smile. He glanced at his bride. But *dannazione*, the girl was no fool. He'd thought it would be so easy to seduce her. He'd seen the kind of life she led—the constant struggle, the deprivation, the fight for survival. Women always fell to him so easily; he'd never once considered that he could propose marriage to Lucia and she would *refuse*.

Her mistake. She'd issued him a challenge. He'd accepted.

And now that he'd kissed her…

Maximo looked at Lucia, sleeping on the sofa. Her ponytail was so disheveled that it barely clung to her head above the cascading dark tendrils. She'd taken off her glasses, and her fresh-scrubbed skin glowed like porcelain.

There was something about her. Some quality beneath the dowdy clothes. A steely strength, a soft vulnerability. She was different from any woman he'd known.

And *that kiss*.

He touched his mouth. He could still feel it. The trembling touch of her lips, the way she'd desperately tried to resist before succumbing in his embrace.…

He took a deep breath, savoring the anticipation. He hadn't been so excited by the prospect of any seduction in a long time.

Perhaps he should have pressed her for more kisses, instead of immediately ordering a car to take them to the airport.

No. He stroked his chin. It was still too soon.

In seduction, as in business, timing was everything.

But he wanted her. And so he'd have her. Why not? Why not add one more layer of pleasure to the whole endeavor? After all, he'd never been married before, and he likely never would be again.

They'd been married with just minutes to spare.

The fact that she didn't trust him only proved her intelligence. He'd deliberately had to distract her before she looked too closely at the prenuptial agreement.

But he'd make sure she lived in luxury and comfort for the rest of her life. Thirty million dollars was nothing. After their divorce, she would receive hundreds more. Too generous of him, perhaps. But he wanted the debt paid in full.

After everything he'd read in the private investigator's report, the neglect Lucia had endured in foster care, the terrible, desperate poverty she'd experienced over the last year, he wanted to make sure he never had to think about it again.

And after their divorce, he would finally be free.

She'd lose her stake in Ferrazzi SpA—but what did she, or any woman, care about running a company? She would be happy buying jewels and clothes and toys for her daughter, entertaining friends at gorgeous parties, buying homes across the world. Whatever she desired. If she wanted a real husband, he'd even find her one.

She would be happy. He'd see to it.

And then he could comfortably forget her, and be able to enjoy his life again. It had been too long since he'd truly enjoyed anything...

The baby suddenly hiccuped. She was sleeping

across her mother's chest, her plump arms flung carelessly over Lucia's shoulders. Such a sweet child. Wentworth really was a fool, Maximo thought. To desert his pregnant lover, and then deny his own daughter…

His jaw hardened. The man deserved what he was about to get. If Lucia had been pregnant with Maximo's child, he would have treated them both like gold.

But that was a ridiculous thought. Giuseppe Ferrazzi would soon be dead. Maximo would write Lucia an enormous check, bid her farewell and go back to his carefree bachelor life.

The world was full of beautiful women. He would never tie himself down to just one. Particularly not to an unstylish twenty-one-year-old with a smart mouth. He preferred his lovers to be more seasoned. More sophisticated. He preferred gorgeous, experienced women who understood the game for what it was.

His attraction for Lucia would not last. He would soon grow tired of her, as he did of every other woman.

Although at the moment, that was hard to imagine.

As if she felt his steady gaze, her eyes fluttered open. For several seconds, she stared at him as if trying to wake up from a dream. Then, careful not to wake the baby sleeping in her arms, she sat up. Rubbing the back of her neck, she gave him a tremulous smile. "How long was I asleep?"

"We'll be landing in a few minutes."

"I slept the whole Atlantic away." She looked down at her sleeping baby. "And so did she. I can hardly believe it, after the way she cried during takeoff. Our first time on a plane," she explained.

No, it's not, he thought. But he said only, "Did you enjoy your flight?"

She looked around the plane, with its luxurious white leather couches, then gave a soft laugh. "It's amazing. Although I can't help but wonder—" she eyed the pristine, snow-white carpet "—who keeps that clean. I have a hard time picturing you with a shampooer."

He returned her grin. "You're right. I have people for that." As if on cue, one of his assistants emerged from the back cabin with a large garment bag. "Lucia, this is Paola Andretti. She's my personal assistant and fashion liaison. She is going to help you."

His short-haired, ultrathin assistant, cutting-edge fashionable as always, smiled down at Lucia pleasantly.

"Help me with what?" Lucia said uneasily.

"Your clothes," he said.

"I like what I'm wearing now!"

Maximo leaned back against his sofa, confident and comfortable in his pressed Italian trousers, his bespoke black shirt, his immaculate black shoes. Quirking an eyebrow, he allowed his eyes to deliberately trace her ratty sweatshirt, her old jeans.

Her pale cheeks became as scarlet as roses.

Good. So she knew. At least that was a start.

"You always want the truth," he said. "*Bene*. The truth is that you have the worst fashion sense I've ever seen. My conglomerate comprises ten luxury brands, including the world's most expensive champagne, accessories and haute couture. You are wearing clothes that barely look fit for dogs to sleep in. No one will ever believe that I am in love with you. From now on, you will wear what I give you."

Her pink mouth, so luscious and full even without lipstick, fell open. Then her expressive eyes narrowed as she snatched up her glasses. "Like hell I will!"

Paola discreetly disappeared to the back cabin of the plane, but Lucy barely noticed. "You can't tell me what to wear!"

He calmly opened a copy of the *Chicago Tribune* to the business page. "Until you learn how to properly dress yourself, I can and I will."

Scowling, she ripped open the garment bag, staring at the supershort purple silk trapeze dress, fishnet stockings and black patent leather boots he'd selected for her. Her jaw dropped.

"You want me to look like a *stripper*?" she said accusingly.

"It is the highest fashion."

"Not for me, it isn't!"

"Do you truly consider yourself to be an arbiter of style?"

She ground her teeth. "This sweatshirt belonged to my mother!"

"Your mother?" he mused, turning his attention back to the business headlines. "Impossible."

"You didn't even know her!"

Abruptly remembering who she was talking about, he put down the newspaper. "Lucia—"

"Call me Lucy!"

"Lucia, you don't seem to realize your new position. My company sets the fashion trends of the world. For the months you are my wife, I expect you to dress with some self-respect."

"Self-respect?" she cried. "Clothes have nothing to do with self-respect! What difference does it make what I wear—except to snobby rich people like you?"

"Ma-ma-ma?" Jabbering as she woke, Chloe stretched in her arms, reaching for her mother's face. In spite of her anger Lucia's face instantly softened as she looked down at her daughter. "Good morning, my baby," she said tenderly, kissing her plump, rosy cheeks. "Did you sleep well?"

Then she straightened in her seat, giving Maximo a hard glare—as if he were an outsider, an interloper, some *stronzo* who would cruelly force a woman to wear designer clothes against her will.

He sighed. Tenting his hands, he leaned forward. "Lucia, *per favore*—"

"No!" Childishly she turned her face away, dropping the purple silk to the floor like discarded rubbish.

He realized he'd hurt her feelings.

Maledizione, he swore to himself. This would require more care than he'd thought.

Leaning forward, he spoke quietly.

"You're a beautiful woman, *cara*. All I want is for the whole world to esteem you as I do. Presenting *la bella figura* will show all of Europe what I already know—that you are a woman unlike any other. A good heart, a fine mind, great strength of will, you are... *bellissima*."

She slowly turned toward him. She wouldn't meet his eyes as she repeated—as if afraid to ask the question, *"Bellissima?"*

"Look at me."

She took a deep breath, then looked up. He leaned across the wide aisle between them.

"Truly." He placed her hands together, enfolding them in his larger ones. "You are—" he kissed the knuckle of her right hand "—truly beautiful—" he opened her trembling left hand and slowly kissed her tender palm "—and I want the whole world to know. Lucia."

"Yes?" she whispered, her dark eyelashes fluttering against her cheek.

"Try the clothes. For me. Won't you?"

"Yes." She rose to her feet so quickly that she took one stumble forward, nearly losing her balance as she held Chloe under one arm. Still looking dazed, she picked up the purple silk.

And Maximo realized he'd made a mistake.

The purple dress would have looked perfect on Esmé or Arabella or any of the other women he'd taken to his bed. But it was all wrong for her.

"I've changed my mind," he said.

"But I—"

"No," he said abruptly. "That dress is not for you. We will delay our arrival at Lake Como to go shopping in Milan." He looked at the squirming baby in her arms. She was still wearing old pajamas. "For both of you."

A smile lit up Lucy's face.

"Oh, Maximo, really?" she exclaimed. "Chloe has outgrown nearly everything she has. I would love new clothes for her. But are you—are you sure you don't mind? About the money, I mean?"

He nearly laughed aloud. Just seeing the joy on his bride's face made her so impossibly beautiful that he wondered why he hadn't thought of taking her shopping before.

"Buy everything you want," he vowed. "If Milan runs out of clothes, we will go to Rome."

"Oh!" she cried, beaming at him. But her face suddenly fell. "But it's New Year's Day. The shops will be closed."

Now he really did laugh. "They will open for me."

"They will?"

"Lucia. Half of them are mine. The other half wish they were."

A shadow suddenly passed over her face. "Like your women," she whispered.

He reached for her hand, pulling her to sit next to him on the white leather sofa. "I have only one wife."

He felt her tremble, and he was tempted to kiss her. Then Chloe, sitting on her mother's lap, cooed happily at him, holding out her arms. Surprised, he picked her up.

The baby dropped her tattered purple hippo and started stretching wildly toward the white carpet. He got the toy for her, then paused, looking down at it. The hippo was a ragged little thing, with one eye missing and its plush fur a muddied brownish-violet. But Chloe was instantly happy when he handed it to her. She waved it around furiously with one hand, laughing with abandon.

And against his will, Maximo remembered the last time he'd held a baby. The smoke. The crackle of the fire. The wail, and then the explosion...

"What's wrong?" Lucy asked suddenly.

He shook his head, scattering the haunting image from his mind. "Nothing."

But his unwilling memory proved the situation was more risky than he'd thought. Somehow Lucia and her baby had broken through his defenses, forcing him to remember everything he was determined to forget.

Seducing Lucia would be dangerous.

But that was all the more reason to do it, he thought. His enjoyment of her company only made it clear that his life of so-called pleasure had been a life without spark.

He wanted her fire. Needed it. Needed *her*.

So he would take her. He'd just have to be constantly on his guard. He wouldn't be vulnerable. He wouldn't open his heart. He would just enjoy her.

And with any luck, he thought, the old man would die the day after his seduction was complete—and he could send her packing.

CHAPTER SEVEN

SITTING in the backseat of the Rolls-Royce, traveling from Milan to Lake Como that afternoon, Lucy barely recognized herself. Or Maximo, for that matter.

What had happened to the selfish, arrogant prince? In the hours since they'd arrived in Italy, Maximo had been nothing but charming. He'd spent the entire morning following her from one exclusive baby boutique to the next, carrying bags, pushing Chloe in a gorgeous new stroller. It was only when the trunk of the Rolls was full of baby clothes that he'd put his foot down and demanded she buy some clothes for herself.

From Prada to Chanel, Versace to Valentino, he'd patiently waited in every store. While Lucy tried on clothes, he had read new books to Chloe until she fell asleep in her stroller. Then, when Lucy blushingly came out of her dressing room, he'd given his verdict on each outfit with a flash of heat in his eyes. And the occasional murmured *"Bellissima."*

At every shop, she'd been flattered and complimented, waited on hand and foot. Her last stop, at the most famous day spa in Milan, she'd had six people waiting on her at once: the first doing her makeup, the second her hair, the third her nails, the fourth her toes, the fifth rubbing her shoulders as the last brought her a *caffè americano*.

Lucy's glasses had been replaced by contacts. Her messy ponytail had been washed, cut and carefully blown into a sleek chignon. Her makeup was natural, artless. Wearing a sophisticated blouse and pencil skirt beneath a belted camel cashmere coat, Lucy had never felt so womanly—or so elegant. Her old glasses, along with necessities for Chloe, were now tucked into her patent leather Ferrazzi carryall.

Her three-thousand-dollar diaper bag.

She crossed her high-heeled ankle boots, stroking the exquisite pearls at her collarbone. Maybe Maximo had a point, she mused. Maybe clothes really could change the way a person felt about herself.

Not that she would ever admit that to him. He was too smug already by half.

"You are magnificent, *cara*," he said, looking at her in amazement.

She blushed, glancing at him over Chloe's baby seat. "I was hoping you'd just say I was passable as your wife."

"Passable? *Dio santo! Sei bellissima.* You are beautiful, *Lucia*."

Lucia. Dressed like this, riding in a limo on the way to an Italian villa, married to a prince, she almost felt like she fit the name. New name. New look. New hope.

It still troubled her that their marriage was timed to last until some poor old man's death. But as Maximo had said, people died every day. The world was a harsh place. Lucy knew that from experience. Her own mother had died when she was twelve, and she'd never known her father.

But now Chloe would never know such a precarious existence. She would be safe and financially secure. And after she spoke to Alex, she'd have a father. Lucy would make sure of it…

She looked at her baby. Buckled into the child seat, Chloe was contentedly gulping down a bottle. Instead of her ratty old pajamas, she wore a pink dress with a rounded collar, thick white tights and white suede boots lined with sheepskin. Her beautiful new Italian wardrobe would last until she was three years old, and each outfit was softer and cuter than the last. Looking at her happy, adorable baby, grateful tears rose to Lucy's eyes.

"Thank you," she whispered. She turned to look at her husband, smiling through the tears. "I can't thank you enough for this."

"For shopping?" he said, sounding surprised. His dark eyebrows lowered. "Don't thank me. I'm starting to regret I ever had the idea. You look far too beautiful. Every man who sees you will want you for himself. In fact," he growled, "I'm beginning to reconsider that sweatshirt."

She looked at him with an intake of breath.

His blue eyes twinkled at her, warm as May sunshine. *He was flirting with her!*

She tried not to respond, to not let it affect her, but it still made her catch her breath. "You're a hard man to please."

"No," he said. "I just want you to be happy."

His gaze was like a pure Italian spring warming her soul. Half-dead flowers unfurled in her heart, basking in his light and heat.

No!

She couldn't be pulled in. She couldn't let him seduce her. She couldn't let him have her body—or her heart. Because when he left her—as he would in a matter of months—she'd be a ruined wreck. Three months. Just three months, and she and Chloe would be safe forever. How hard could it be to resist a man for three months?

Very hard, when the man was Prince Maximo d'Aquilla...

Biting her lip, she turned to look out the window as they traveled the snowy single-lane road. Even in Italy, winter held sway. But this winter was different than it'd been in Chicago. Warmer, for one thing. Lake Como was an Italian winter fairyland. The limo sped down the slender dark ribbon of a street into a village clinging to mountains. Snow sparkled in the sun like diamonds, on the edge of a sapphire lake.

"Aquillina," he said. "My home."

She looked out her window in wonder. Villagers were strolling down the main street in the sunshine, chatting with each other in front of charming, decorated shops. Bright-eyed old men raised their caps in greeting as the Rolls-Royce passed by. Young mothers pushing strollers pointed out the car to their rosy-cheeked babies. A group of boys, six or seven years old, chased the limo down the street, shouting after them with hearty cheers.

Lucy looked at Maximo in wonder. "It's beautiful."

He smiled at her, and his eyes caressed her face, lingering on her lips. "I'm glad you like it."

Her whole body vibrated under his gaze. *Stop it*, she told her body furiously. *He's nothing to you!* But her body laughed at her orders, as uncontrollable as a rebellious child. With Maximo so close to her, the roomy backseat felt way too small.

She swallowed, looking away. "Are we almost to— what did you call it?"

"The Villa Uccello. It's been my family's home for many generations. We lost it briefly when I was a child, but now it is mine again." He gave her a brief smile. "And for the next few months, it is yours."

Pushing her empty bottle away, Chloe accidentally knocked her purple hippo out of her lap. She started to whine. Maximo and Lucy both reached to the floor at the same time, their fingertips brushing together over the plush fur.

Lucy yanked her hand back as if she'd been burned. Hiding a smug smile, he handed the stuffed animal to Chloe.

"Hold on to your toy more carefully," he admonished the baby. Lucy frowned in surprise. It was one thing for him to take that tone with her, but how dare he order her child to…

Then she saw Chloe smile, reaching for his nose. Maximo crossed his eyes playfully, and the baby's laughter rang like the chimes of bells. He laughed with her, and his eyes were warm, crinkling at the sides.

It took Lucy's breath away.

"You're good with her," she blurted out. "Do you have children of your own?"

His face instantly shuttered.

"No," he said brusquely, sitting back. "I've never been married."

"But that doesn't mean—"

"I would not have a child without being married to the mother. That would be irresponsible."

She flushed, feeling the sting of his words. He obviously thought she'd been irresponsible to get pregnant.

And she had been, she thought with a lump in her throat. She'd trusted Alex's pretty words and promises of love. She'd made excuses for him—justifying why, after proposing to her with a big diamond ring and getting her pregnant, he'd suddenly been reluctant to pick a wedding date.

She'd been so stupid. She'd thought she'd found a real man, a real home, a real family after so many years of being alone. And for that, she gave up everything. She threw away the college scholarship she'd worked so hard to win, tossing aside her plans to be a school librarian, teaching children to love books.

Blinking back tears, she looked away. She could never let herself forget the pain—never let herself be vulnerable and weak like that again. She was her daughter's only protection. Her only support.

"Children need a father," Maximo said, and she again felt the sting of blame.

Suddenly furious, she shook her head. "Do you think I don't know that?" she bit out. "I grew up without a father. My mother moved us from place to place, and when she died I was totally alone. Do you think I want that for Chloe? It's why I—"

"Why what?" he said sharply.

She bit her lip. "Why I think even a selfish, shallow father is better than none at all."

"Wentworth doesn't deserve to be her father." Maximo's lip curled. "He fled America to avoid taking even the most basic responsibility."

She swallowed, pressing her fingernails into her palms. "But he's her father, Maximo. She has no siblings. No cousins. No one. If anything ever happens to me, I need to know she's safe, that she'll be loved and protected."

"Not by Wentworth." Maximo's gaze was stony. "He's lost his chance."

She stared at him. "What do you mean?"

"Alexander Wentworth is going to sign away his parental rights to Chloe and you are going to convince him to do it."

Lucy stared at him in shock.

"Make Alex sign away his parental rights?" she gasped. "No! Whatever he's done to me, he's still her father!"

"You promised to obey, Lucia."

"Sure—about stupid things, like who gets the remote control! Not something like this!"

Maximo's face was cold. "Unless Wentworth's rights are terminated, he could decide to challenge you for custody of your daughter at any time."

"Custody?" She gave a harsh, bitter laugh. "I'm just praying to convince him to give her an occasional phone call, or a gift for her birthday!"

He looked at her for a long moment. "He will never care about her. He only cares about himself. That makes him dangerous."

"He wouldn't try to take Chloe away from me!"

"You never thought he would abandon you, either. Excuse me if I say you're a poor judge of character." But before she could get hurt by this rude statement, his gaze softened. "Perhaps because you believe the best of people. An admirable quality. One I've never shared."

"Well, I've never believed the best of *you*," she muttered.

He ignored her. "Wentworth might try to use Chloe against you for reasons you cannot imagine. To blackmail you out of an inheritance, for example."

She laughed incredulously. "What inheritance?"

"Remove him from your life. Either you do it the easy way—or I'll do it the hard way."

"Why do you care? You don't give a damn about me—or Chloe!"

"You're wrong." His dark blue eyes focused on hers. "You are both under my protection now. Do you not understand what that means? I must keep you safe. And he is a danger to you both."

"But Chloe needs a father. You said so yourself!"

"If he asks to be her father, it won't be because he's looking out for her interests. Just his own."

"But—"

"You will obey me, Lucia." His voice held a steely edge. "I know what is best."

He expected her to submit to his will. Of course he

did. Women didn't say "no" to Prince Maximo d'Aquilla, did they?

But Lucy couldn't cut Alex out of Chloe's life. She couldn't make a choice that her daughter might someday regret. But under Maximo's commanding gaze, the best she could do was look away. She scowled at the passing landscape.

"What is that?" she said suddenly.

"What?"

"That." She pointed at a run-down mansion on the edge of the village. It must have once been an elegant villa; but the windows were all boarded up, the stucco walls falling into ruin, the yard overgrown. "Who lives there?"

His whole body sat up straight in his seat, on the alert. "Why?"

"I don't know," she said, wondering why he seemed so tense. "It just looks…out of place."

His jaw tightened. "An old man lives there. A man nobody cares about."

She frowned. "But surely, if he's elderly, someone should…"

"Forget him," he said sharply.

His fierce anger made her draw back in hurt and confusion. They sat in silence until the limo finally pulled through a wrought-iron gate.

"*Bene,*" he said shortly. "We're here."

The limo stopped, and the chauffeur opened her door.

She saw an enormous multitiered villa, white as a neoclassical wedding cake, surrounded by elaborate gardens overlooking a crystal-blue lake. Put all together, it was white and blue and wide as heaven…

"This is my home," he said quietly. "The Villa Uccello."

Then she saw the crowds of people lining the front steps.

"Who are they?" she whispered.

"Servants. Neighbors. Here to meet you." Maximo unbuckled Chloe from her car seat, smiling down at the baby warmly. "And to celebrate your birthday, little one."

Chloe chattered and waved her hippo in reply as he lifted her from the car.

Maximo had remembered Chloe's birthday? Lucy rose from the car. She forgot all about the decrepit villa, the wedding-cake Villa Uccello, even forgot the crowds of people waiting for her.

All she could see was her baby, happy in Maximo's arms.

Why hadn't Alex ever held Chloe like that? Why had he never held her *at all*? He hadn't cared about her birthday—he hadn't even cared about her *birth*. He'd ignored his own child, brushed her off like an embarrassment, sent her pictures back unopened. He had abandoned her to struggle—left her to starve.

Maximo, though unrelated by blood, was already acting more like a father to Chloe than Alex ever had. Unlike Alex with his sweet words and faithless proposal of marriage, Maximo d'Aquilla hadn't bothered to explain a damn thing. In fact, he'd barely bothered about the niceties of proposing—he'd just married her practically by force.

But he'd taken both Lucy and Chloe under his wing. He'd taken her away from desperate hardship, made her his princess and brought her to Italy. He'd made sure she and Chloe would be secure for the rest of their lives.

Maximo d'Aquilla was a man of deeds, not words. And unlike Alex, he told the *truth*. He'd even had the decency to warn her never to love him…

No problem, she told herself. She wouldn't love a playboy. Couldn't.

But she couldn't prevent the memory of their kiss last night from replaying in her mind. She could still feel his mouth against hers. Demanding. Insisting. Possessing her against her will… Making her want and demand and insist on possessing him in return…

Maximo held out his free hand to her.

"Come, my bride."

And she obeyed.

As they walked up the steps to the glamorous, palatial villa, people followed them inside the ten-foot-high doors, chattering happily in Italian. A smiling maid took her coat as three footmen carried bags from the car, and the chauffeur drove the Rolls-Royce to park it in the mews.

I've entered a fairy tale, she thought in wonder. Just like Cinderella's castle.

Past the foyer, they entered a large salon with a high ceiling, covered with frescoes of cherubic angels and embracing Renaissance lovers. Lucy sucked in her breath at the sheer size of it—and the elegance. This *palace* was to be her home for the next three months?

But there was more. Past the antique furniture in the salon, above the soaring marble fireplace, she saw a big silken banner with handpainted words.

Happy First Birthday. Buon compleanno, Chloe!

The room was decorated with hundreds of pink flowers and balloons. Next to the fireplace, she saw a mountain of gift-wrapped presents. Presiding over the gifts was a stuffed giraffe nearly as tall as Lucy wearing a pink bow. And on the table behind the elegant uphol-stered sofa, there was a pink birthday cake, six tiers high.

Maximo had done this all—for Chloe. A child he'd only met yesterday.

Lucy stopped as tears rushed to her eyes. Yesterday, she'd had neither gifts nor a cake for her beloved daughter. Today, everything had changed.

"Thank you," she whispered, clutching his hand. "I can't believe you did this for Chloe."

"No." He looked at her. "I did it for you."

His blue gaze went through her soul. How had he known the deepest longing of her heart? Prince Maximo d'Aquilla really was too good to be true.

But as happy tears streamed down her face unchecked, and she was trying to think of a way to express the depth of her gratitude and joy, his hand tightened on hers.

Turning to face the crowd of people in the salon, he spoke in English, his voice commanding and clear. "My dear friends, thank you for coming today. Allow me to introduce my bride. After twenty years, she has finally come home. Allow me to present...Lucia Ferrazzi."

CHAPTER EIGHT

LUCIA Ferrazzi?

Lucy nearly gasped aloud.

Ferrazzi—as in Ferrazzi handbags?

As in the company he was trying to gain through hostile takeover?

She looked at him, the man who just a moment ago had seemed too good to be true. And all her gratitude and joy evaporated like smoke.

"Lucia Ferrazzi!" The people in the salon, perhaps fifty or sixty in total, burst into excited rapid-fire speech in both English and Italian. "Lucia Ferrazzi!" A white-haired old woman in the corner suddenly burst into tears, crying above the din, *"Bambina mia…"*

And Lucy felt sick.

"I want to talk to you," she ground out to Maximo. "Right now."

"Later." He gave a charming, gracious smile. "Greet your guests and friends. Some of them have waited for you for decades."

"But I'm not—" she gasped as she was dragged from

him and Chloe, pulled away by the tide of people rushing forward to embrace her. They had tears in their eyes as they cried out her name. But it wasn't her name, Lucy Abbott, that they were crying with such wonder and amazement and shock. It was Lucia Ferrazzi. *Miracolo*, they repeated over and over.

As she was hugged by a crowd of excited strangers, Lucy glared across the salon at Maximo. Watching him smile and joke with the villagers' children, he looked so handsome and wonderful that it made her heart ache. As if he had no idea of Lucy's torment, he sat down calmly on the floor with Chloe in his lap and helped her open her first birthday present. He ripped the pink wrapping paper, pulling it down just enough so the baby could reach up and rip the rest.

Discovering a train set in the box, Chloe chortled happily. Maximo looked up at Lucy and smiled.

And she *hated* him. Fiercely. Savagely.

He'd almost made her believe. Against her will, he'd almost convinced her he was an honest man. When the truth was that he was an even bigger liar than Alex.

The prince was a cheat.

A *fraud*.

The white-haired old woman who'd sobbed in the crowd threw her arms around Lucy, nearly knocking her over with the impact of the embrace.

"Mia bambina," the old woman gasped. *"Che meravigliosa notizia!"* Her eyes were rheumy with weeping. Lucy tried haplessly to separate herself as the woman continued to babble in Italian. Even if Lucy had spoken Italian, she didn't think she would have understood a

word as the woman gasped and sobbed through every syllable. The woman choked out a question. She looked at Lucy, her eyes begging for an answer.

Lucy shook her head. "I'm sorry, I don't speak Italian," she said. "And I'm not who you think—"

"Annunziata was your nurse," a voice said in English behind her. "Your *bambinaia*."

Glancing back, Lucy saw a girl who couldn't have been more than eighteen or nineteen. She was petite, slender and extremely pretty, with masses of dark hair and olive skin. The girl continued, "She is asking to know if you have had a happy life. She says after you disappeared as a baby, she prayed every night that you escaped the fire. And now she has seen a miracle. You are here."

"What fire?" Lucy asked, wondering if the girl was another of Maximo's mistresses. Trying not to wonder, because for some reason it made her hurt all over. "What are you talking about?"

The old woman chattered rapidly, embracing her. Then, as if her emotions were too much, she ran away, fleeing with a sob.

"Don't you know?" The girl's expressive blue eyes widened. "You're famous here. When you were one year old, your father skidded his car off a cliff and it exploded in a fire. Your parents died at once, but you were never found. Everyone thought you were dead. Except for your grandfather."

"Grandfather?" Lucy repeated, troubled.

"*Sì.*" The girl gave a brief half smile. "Although last month he finally petitioned the courts to have you declared dead. But I think that has more to do with him needing money than really believing you were…where are you going?"

"To kill my husband," Lucy said, clenching her hands into fists.

"What?" the girl gasped.

First a sweet old lady, now a grandfather? How many people was Maximo willing to hurt to gain control of Ferrazzi?

Lucy ground her teeth. "I'm going to get my daughter away from that *liar*."

The girl's hand grasped her shoulder. "Did I say something wrong?"

"No." Lucy's eyes narrowed as she looked at her husband. "You said exactly the right thing."

Maximo stood out above the crowd, a handsome, dark giant of a man. Everyone deferred to him. Everyone admired him. He was twice as handsome as blond, slender Alex. And twice the liar.

The more handsome the man, she thought, the more selfish and cold the heart.

She'd wondered why he rescued her from the cold Chicago winter. Now she knew. Due to some chance resemblance, he meant to use her to get control of the Ferrazzi company. He thought he could trick people into believing she was that poor missing baby. People like the gullible, heartbroken old nurse. Like the baby's grandfather, who must have suffered unimaginable grief. When they discovered the truth, it would be like losing that baby all over again.

But what did her husband care about that, so long as he got what he wanted?

Maximo met her gaze over the crowd and gave her a sensual smile. It made her shiver—and she stiffened her spine. If he thought that he could seduce her into silence with his dangerously sexy charm—if he thought he could buy her integrity with his power and wealth, he was dead wrong...

He *was* wrong, wasn't he?

Lucy took a deep breath. Of course he was wrong. She'd consented to sell three months of her time. For her daughter's sake, she might be willing to do more. She didn't care about her own life. Just Chloe's. For her daughter, she would sacrifice anything—even her own life.

But hurting innocent people? To benefit her own child? That was entirely different. That was evil. Lucy wasn't such a monster.

Some things were more important than financial security. Her own mother had taught her that.

Lucy took a deep breath. "I'm going to go tell everyone that their prince is a big fat liar."

"No! You can't!"

Lucy straightened her shoulders. "Look, I'm sure you're in love with him just like every other woman in the world, but the truth is—"

"I'm not his mistress!" the girl exclaimed, sounding insulted. "I'm Amelia, his cousin. But I do love him. Maximo has always taken care of me and my mother. I don't know why you're so angry, but you must at least give him the respect of speaking with him in private! It's your duty as his wife!"

"My duty as his wife!" Lucy repeated in shock. Had

they traveled to Lake Como in a time machine, and gone back to the nineteenth century?

With an expressive sweep of her hand, the Italian girl indicated the party decorations, the cake, the presents, the laughing children. "My cousin must be deeply in love with you. He will therefore forgive you—"

"Forgive *me*!" Lucy gasped, dumbfounded.

"But he is a proud man, and if you humiliate him in front of the whole village your marriage will never be the same. Don't destroy your life together before it has even begun!"

Amelia's blue eyes were pleading. She didn't know that Lucy's relationship with Maximo was a marriage of convenience. She actually thought that Maximo had married her for love.

Exactly what he wanted everyone to think.

Right, Lucy thought, her throat choked with bitterness and hurt. *As if he'd ever be vulnerable that way in a million years.*

But looking around at all the bright eyes of the villagers, hearing the happy laughter of the children, she took a deep breath. She would restrain herself for their sakes, not his. "Fine," she ground out. "But you can't expect me to just stand here while he's telling these *lies*—"

"Let me take you on a tour of the villa," Amelia suggested brightly. "I'll get your baby."

But a minute later, when she placed a squirming Chloe in Lucy's arms, the baby didn't seem entirely happy about it. She kept peeking over Lucy's shoulder, reaching her pudgy arms toward Maximo, whimpering and shaking her hippo in his direction.

But Lucy was afraid to even look back at him. Afraid if she saw him, she'd scream out her anger and hurt. Or she'd rush across the salon and stand on her tiptoes (or possibly get a chair) to slap him hard across the face.

But why? Why did she feel so hurt? How could she possibly feel so betrayed, when she'd known from the beginning she couldn't trust a handsome man who seemed too good to be true?

"Such a sweet baby," Amelia said softly, stroking Chloe's downy hair as they left the salon and started down the hall. "Maximo thinks I am wasting my time at university. He tells me to find a nice man and settle down." She gave an impish grin. "I've always told him that he had to get married first! But now he's finally found you, I no longer have an excuse…"

"For heaven's sake, stay in school!" Lucy blurted out. "Love ruins everything!"

Amelia stopped above her on the wide staircase, looking down at her in surprise. "But you love my cousin. Surely you wouldn't allow one moment of anger to make you forget that? Maximo is a great man. Bossy, *certamente*, but only to protect the people he loves." She stroked Chloe's hair again. "Whatever he has done to make you angry, I'm sure it is because he loves you, Lucia."

Lucy felt a sudden lump in her throat. She envied the girl's pure heart. Amelia loved her cousin and believed the best of him. Just the way Lucy had once had faith in people.

But looking at the girl's idealistic, shining face, Lucy couldn't take that same faith from her. Swallowing, she turned away. "Tell me about the villa."

"Look at this room first." Amelia stopped in front of the third door on the left of the second-floor hallway. "The nursery."

Lucy couldn't believe her eyes.

Just yesterday, she'd thought the Drake Hotel had the most elegant bedrooms she'd ever seen.

But this nursery was a pure extravagant fantasy. Wide windows overlooked the rosy twilight as the sun fell behind the lake and distant hills. The carpet was thick and pink, perfect for a crawling baby who would soon learn to walk. The crib was white with pale pink bedding. On the far wall, a built-in white bookshelf was lined with hundreds of children's books. Brand-new toys cascaded from a white antique toy chest, and in the closet, carefully unpacked by unseen hands, were the adorable baby clothes she'd bought in Milan.

But their morning in Milan, the most fantastic morning of her life, had been nothing more than bribery, an attempt to convince Lucy to pretend to be the Ferrazzi girl.

Chloe saw the toys and started wriggling desperately, wanting to be put down on the floor to crawl and explore and play.

Lucy's throat hurt.

This baby nursery was everything Chloe deserved. Everything Lucy wished she could provide for her. It was a fairy tale, and she desperately wished she could give it to her daughter.

But then she'd have to stay married to an ogre. No, worse: she'd be an ogre herself, hurting other people just to keep her own child in silks and toys.

"I'm sorry," Lucy whispered, pressing her cheek to her baby's. She felt like crying. "I can't give you this."

"Ugh. It's getting dark." Amelia turned the light switch, illuminating a wrought-iron chandelier that was a fantasy confection of white and pink flowers. "That's better." She held out her arms for Chloe. "Can we play a bit? She's my second cousin now, and we need to get acquainted!"

Chloe eagerly shook her hippo at Amelia.

Lucy knew she shouldn't allow them to be friends, not even for a second. She had to leave this place. Tell everyone that she was not Lucia Ferrazzi. She'd be unable to accept the hush money he'd offered her in the prenup, since her conscience wouldn't allow her to earn it. She'd take her daughter back to Chicago. Back to their cold, threadbare apartment, to their ripped-up old carpet and sparse secondhand clothes. Back to the desperation of working multiple dead-end jobs, never seeing her daughter, praying the apartment manager would give her time to catch up on rent.

Maybe, if she begged Darryl, he would let her have her old job back at the gas station.

"Lucia?"

Fighting tears, she gave Chloe to Amelia without a word.

"That's your room over there," the girl said, nodding toward a door on the other side before she sat down on the floor near the toys. She smiled down at Chloe, showing her a baby-size grand piano. "Maximo knew you would want it to connect directly to Chloe's room, so he had it refurbished for you."

Lucy had a fantasy bedroom as well?

She knew she shouldn't look. *Mustn't.* Why give herself a taste of what she'd never have? In a few hours, she would return to Chicago, to the real life that fate had decreed for her. Why even allow herself a vision of what she'd lost? Why make her heart yearn for the fantasy?

She looked at the closed door.

Right or wrong, she had to see it. Even if it hurt. She couldn't spend the rest of her life wondering...

Leaving Amelia and Chloe playing with toys on the carpet, she pushed open the door.

It was dark.

Only the light from Chloe's room traced the unlit crystal chandelier hanging from the soaring ceiling. She saw blackout curtains drawn across the windows. But the bedroom was huge, in white and blue toile, like exquisite china. In the far corner she saw a dark wood vanity, obviously an antique; multicolored leather-bound books lined the opposite wall.

She walked farther into the room.

Inside the walk-in closet, she saw the exquisite designer clothes and shoes she'd bought in Milan, organized neatly. On the other side of the closet were tailored suits and men's shoes.

This fantasy bedroom hadn't been meant for Lucy alone.

A voice, low and grim, spoke from behind her.

"You disobeyed me. *Again.*"

Maximo!

But as she whirled around to face him, the open door slammed, plunging the room into darkness. She heard slow, heavy footsteps against the carpet, heard the rapid beating of her own pounding heart.

"You are a liar," she gasped, trying desperately to see where he was, "and I'm going back to Chicago."

A growl came from the shadows, and suddenly, his body was against hers. Holding her captive, he held her tight against his heat in the darkness.

CHAPTER NINE

THE bedroom was too dark to see his face, but Lucy felt every inch of him as he crushed her against his body. He was so much larger than her, so much stronger. This flesh-and-blood prince, a man of shadows, uncontrollable, undeniable...

"You're not going anywhere but my bed."

"No—" She struggled in his arms but to no avail. His lips descended ruthlessly upon hers.

His kiss was passionate. Unyielding. In the darkness, he seduced her to his will beneath an onslaught of fire. She sagged against him, helpless to resist, helpless even to object. His lips were warm, the taste of his mouth as sweet as molten candy. His body felt good against hers. Too good.

If something feels too good to be true, it's a lie...

With her last drop of self-control, Lucy shoved him away. Grabbing the nearby curtains, she pulled with all her might.

Violet-gray twilight flooded the room, but it was enough. She was safe. Daylight, the bane of any creature of the night, would cause Maximo to lose his strange power over her.

Wouldn't it?

"Lucia. Look at me."

She took a deep breath, then slowly turned her head. *She'd been wrong.*

The weak winter twilight was no defense against his supernatural power. He was still as tall as ever, as dark, as handsome. And the expression in his searing blue gaze as he scorched her body was…hungry.

"You've disobeyed me for the last time."

"You're right." She raised her chin defiantly. "Because I'm going to tell everyone that you're a liar, and leave you—ah!"

He'd crossed to her in two steps, grabbing her by the shoulders. "It's time you learned you cannot constantly accuse me of lying." He pushed her against the wall of curtains, trapping her. Slowly he stroked up her body. "Not without punishment."

She felt his featherlight touch against her belly, between her breasts. She leaned back against the wall, desperately fighting her desire.

"I won't lie for you," she gasped. "I won't pretend I'm that poor lost Ferrazzi girl. I won't let the people who loved her suffer. Not for money. Not for anything."

He stroked her cheek, raising her chin, forcing her to look in his eyes.

"You," he said, "are Lucia Ferrazzi."

Lucy, some exotic long-lost Italian heiress?

"No!" She pulled away. "I'm Lucy Abbott. A regular girl from Illinois. Any other claim is ridiculous!"

"Isn't that what you called my claim to be a prince—'ridiculous'? And you were wrong," he whispered in her ear. "Dead wrong."

He drew away. She realized she'd been holding her breath, and angrily exhaled. "I won't let you pass me off as some long-lost Ferrazzi heiress. Even if I did, it wouldn't work. If anyone digs into my records in Chicago, they'll find out who I am!"

"*Sì,*" he agreed.

His fearlessness bewildered her. "Aren't you afraid they'll discover the truth?"

"The truth is—" he put his hands on her shoulders and looked down at her "—you *are* the Ferrazzi heir. And you're the only liar in the room, with your promise to honor and obey." He glanced back at the bed, then turned back to face her. "What will it take to make you believe I am telling you the truth?"

She trembled, looking at the enormous bed.

How many of his kisses would it take for her to lose her soul?

His first kiss had made her lose all reason.

His second kiss had made her fall into his arms, breathless and yielding in his embrace.

What next?

Two destructive kisses.

She had to make sure he never had the chance for a third.

"You can burn the prenup," she said. "Because I'm not going to pretend to be that girl. I'd rather be out on the street!"

"Peccato." He traced her tender bottom lip with his finger. "You're staying here with me."

Her lip tingled where he touched. She could feel the pressure of his kiss still reverberating through her body. She could still feel his mouth, strong and insistent, spreading hers, his tongue plundering her own. One more kiss like that might make her surrender everything she believed in. She'd done it once before, hadn't she? And Maximo was twice the temptation that Alex had ever been.

He had twice the potential for devastation...

Turning her head, she forced him to release her. As she fought to catch her breath, her gaze fell upon a jeweled brush and comb on a silver tray, resting on the dark wood vanity.

"Those are yours, *cara*," he said quietly. "Everything I have is yours. For as long as you are mine."

"I'm not yours!"

"No," he agreed. Standing behind her, he put his arms around her shoulders. "But you will be. Very soon."

With a shuddering breath, she closed her eyes. She wanted so much to lean against him, to let herself go. The heat from his body seemed to come in waves, pulling her like the sea, drawing her to drown in the waves.

As if he knew her weakness, he pulled her back against his muscled chest. "The tray is all that's left of my family's fortune."

"What happened to it?" she breathed, trying to gather strength to pull away.

"Someone ruined us. When I was five, we had

English tutors, horses, fine cars. This villa." He looked around the room. "By the time I was twelve, he'd taken everything. And more."

She looked up at him in the mirror. His face was closed off, silhouetted with shadow against the last flickers of purple twilight.

"What else did he take?" she whispered.

He abruptly released her.

"It was a long time ago."

His tone was like ice. Obviously the subject was closed.

And Lucy suddenly felt desperately sorry for him—this man that only minutes before she'd thought an ogre.

She impulsively snatched the silver hairbrush from the tray. "You always know everything, don't you?" She held it up with a forced laugh, trying to lighten his mood. "I lost my favorite hairbrush last week. How did you know I needed this?"

He paused, then looked at her in the mirror.

"You didn't lose your hairbrush," he said. "My men took it."

She turned to gape at him. "What?"

His strong, tall form was silhouetted in front of the fading light. "I needed your hair to run a DNA test in Rome. I ordered my men to break into your apartment."

A ripple of cold ricocheted through her body, sending ice down her spine.

"You—broke into my apartment? You stole my *hair-brush*?"

He pushed her toward the bed. "Sit down."

"I spent an hour looking for that hairbrush!" Although that wasn't the point. Trembling with rage, feeling completely violated, she cried, "You sent some seedy body-guard into my home?"

"Sit down!"

He didn't even raise his voice, but her knees weakened of their own accord. She fell onto the bed, despising the power he had over her. Tears sprang to her eyes.

"You shouldn't have done it." Her shoulders shook. "You never should have done it."

"I had to know," he said quietly. "Your grandfather had petitioned to have you declared legally dead." He gave a brief, grim smile. "On the first of January, the shares from your trust fund would have reverted to his control."

"So it's true? I really have a grandfather?" she whispered, dazed. "Do I have cousins? Siblings?"

He stared at her for a moment. "I'm sorry. Just your grandfather, and he does not deserve to be called your family."

She looked up at him in shock.

"He's the one, isn't he? The old man whose death you're waiting for?"

He looked away from her.

"Oh my God, what could he possibly have done?" Then she knew, and sucked in her breath. "He's the one who ruined your family?"

"I do not wish to speak of it."

"But he's my grandfather!"

"He's a stranger to you."

"He's my blood!"

"You will stay away from him, Lucia." His voice was sharp as steel, cutting through her with the brutality of a sword. "Speak with him once—just once—and our contract will be void."

Meaning no marriage. No thirty million dollars. And now that she'd had a taste of the fairy tale, both for herself and for Chloe, she found it hard to imagine giving it up.

"You will obey me in this. Nonnegotiable." His eyes narrowed. "Do I have your word?"

She swallowed, then took a deep breath. He waited.

"All right," she finally muttered.

But it wasn't all right. It wasn't right at all. How could she turn her back on her own grandfather? How could she just wait for him to die, without getting to know him? Without loving him, and giving him the chance to love her—and Chloe?

The air in the darkened bedroom had grown decidedly chilly. She bit her lip. "But if I really am that baby..."

He folded his arms. *"Sì?"*

"Who saved me from that fire after the accident? Who took me to the United States?"

"No one knows," he said coldly. "Connie Abbott was an American tourist staying at my aunt's *pensione* when you disappeared. I heard her say she longed for a child. Perhaps she took you."

She had the sudden feeling that he was keeping something from her. But before she could put her finger on the feeling, she realized what he'd said.

Her mother—a baby thief?

"No! My mother would never—"

She covered her mouth with her hands.

How many times had Connie woken her up in the

middle of the night—switching schools, jobs and apartments from Evanston to Lincoln to Chicago? Her mother had been a family-practice doctor—Lucy had found the M.D. degree buried in her mother's papers—but she'd insisted on taking low-paying, low-profile jobs. Almost as if she were trying to stay invisible. Almost as if for all those years, Connie had been looking over her shoulder, afraid someone would find them and take her child away—

"No." Lucy took a deep breath. "You have no proof."

"Not of how you ended up being raised as her daughter. But I do have proof of your identity." Turning on a small light, he took some papers from his desk. He sat next to her on the bed, his hard thigh pressing against her leg.

She looked up at him, holding her breath.

His lips curved as if he knew the effect he had on her. He probably did. For a man like Maximo, making women ache with desire came naturally as breathing. He was a playboy, wasn't he? He'd no doubt left a trail of broken hearts around the world, while he himself remained careless and free, always seeking his next pleasure.

She envied his cold heart.

"Here." He handed her the papers. "The results of your DNA test. There can be no doubt. You are the long-lost daughter of Narsico and Graziella Ferrazzi."

Her eyes flickered over the scientific jargon, but she couldn't focus on the words. A teardrop plopped noisily onto the top page.

Her mother wasn't her mother.

Her mother had stolen her away from her real family…

Memories of Connie's hugs, her comfort after every

scraped knee, her cookies after school, her homemade ornaments on the Christmas tree, her laughter and love, all pierced Lucy like a betrayal. When she'd lost her mother nine years ago, she'd thought it was the worst pain she would ever experience in her life.

She'd been wrong.

Her mother had known she was dying, but she'd still selfishly kept her secret to the grave. Rather than send Lucy back to Italy, to a grandfather who loved her, she'd left her daughter to languish for six years in foster care, neglected, ignored. Desperate for someone—anyone—to love her.

"She was never my mother," she whispered. "All those years, she said she loved me and she…lied to me. She—"

Then she remembered the last night in the hospital before her mother had died. They'd watched a movie about Italy, and her mother had tried desperately to speak. She'd told Lucy to go to Italy. *She'd told her to go.*

But she'd died before she could explain why.

Lucy closed her eyes, remembering everything about the woman she'd loved more than life. "Mom," she whispered.

Holding the damning DNA results against her chest, she leaned back on the bed, holding her knees tightly. She cried, only dimly aware of Maximo beside her on the bed, comforting her body with his own.

"Chloe!"

Lucy awoke with a start, gasping her daughter's name in a panic. Sitting straight up in bed, it took her a moment to realize where she was: her bedroom at the Villa Uccello. She'd fallen asleep! Only the dying embers of firelight, coupled with the moon's pale shimmer through the wide windows, lit the flickering shadows of the room.

"Chloe's safe," a voice said from the darkness. "Sleeping."

Slowly she turned. Maximo was lying next to her on the bed. He was still dressed, apparently wide-awake. As if he'd been keeping watch over her all night.

"Amelia gave her dinner and tucked her into bed," he said. "She's in the nursery. Go see."

Jumping out of bed, Lucy ran across the room. She opened the connecting door and held herself still until she heard her daughter's steady, even breathing in the darkness. Quietly she closed the door.

Maximo had told the truth. Lucy looked at him in the firelit shadows.

"You stayed with me while I slept. All this time."

"*Sì.*"

"Why?"

"You're my wife."

She shook her head. She'd already cried so much, she had no tears left.

"I'm not your wife. I'm your trust fund," she said bitterly.

"Lucia, come back to bed."

Bed?

She had taken that path once before. Desperate for love, desperate to belong to someone, she grabbed her first chance and held on with all her might. A handsome man. An enormous bed. Soft, tousled sheets. Whispered promises of pleasure and comfort. Luring her—tempting her to her own destruction.

She wouldn't make that mistake again. *Never again.*

Maximo reached his hand out to her, palm up. She stared at his wide, powerful hand, so inviting in its pretense of vulnerability. "Lucia—"

"Stay away from me!" she shouted. "I don't care how well you kiss, or how kind you can be!"

As she spoke the words, she discovered that she had some tears left after all. Folding her arms, she turned toward the fireplace, watching the dying, crackling flames as she willed the tears away.

She heard him get up. Heard him come close behind her. He reached for her chin, forcing her to look at him.

Maximo's eyes were dark as a midnight sea. His chin was dark with stubble, but he still looked handsome and oh, so dangerous in his sharply cut black shirt and trousers. His sensual mouth curved in a smile as he stroked her tears away.

"I'm not a kind man, *cara*," he said. "Do not believe that. But I have seen something in you I admire—the way you insist on the truth. So I will tell you this. Sooner or later, you are going to fall to me. You will come willingly to my bed."

"I won't—"

"You will feel great pleasure. But do not mistake that for love. Choose to love me, and I will break your heart. That is what happens to all foolish women who do not heed my warning. I do not wish it to happen to you."

Her whole body trembled.

"But you are different from the others. You will listen. And obey." He twined a finger around a dark tendril of hair that had escaped her chignon. "You are too intelligent to mistake pleasure for love. Too honest. You know your own soul, and mine."

She felt his touch cascading electricity up and down her body. In the dark bedroom, lit only by the flickering embers of firelight, they were alone. And all her pounding emotions cried out for the physical release of his embrace.

Oh, this was dangerous. So dangerous.

His gaze traced her full, swollen lips. She wanted him to touch her all over. Her nipples were hard, her skin hot. She wanted him to toss her on the bed and make her feel, for just one moment, like she was truly loved. Even if it was a lie...

"Is it really possible to have sex without love?" she whispered.

He stared at her for a moment in the firelight.

"Let me show you."

Turning, he picked up the silver hairbrush from the tray. He took her unresisting hand and led her back to the bed.

No, she tried to say, but her lips wouldn't form the word.

He set her down on the edge of the enormous bed, sitting behind her. With his long, thick fingers, he pulled her dark hair out of the chignon. Slowly he used the brush, softly stroking her hair.

She shivered. Across the room, she could see their reflection in the vanity mirror. What would that mirror reveal if she followed her desire? If she pushed him back against the bed and kissed him hard on the mouth? What would their reflection show if she pressed the softness of her body against his strength, and told him what he somehow already knew—that she was his?

In the intimate portrait of the mirror, she could see the firelight glowing on her skin, on the silver brush, on the sharp lines of his cheekbone and jaw. They looked like any newly married couple on their honeymoon. Protected from the winter's cold, their bedroom was a candle in the dark, bursting with warmth and light.

She clasped her hands together tightly, staring down at the white knuckles of her fingers. The gentle pleasure of the brush stroking her hair was intolerable. She wanted him so badly that she could hardly bear the sweet agony of remaining still.

She had to stop this. Now.

"Stop."

Instantly the brush stilled.

She closed her eyes. Telling herself it would just be for a moment, she leaned back against his chest. Putting the brush aside, he wrapped his arms around her. For one exquisite moment, she allowed herself to feel safe and warm, encircled by his protective embrace.

Not protective, she realized.

Deadly. Poisonous.

"I can't do this," she whispered. "I can't."

He turned her against him on the bed. His face was darkly handsome, and when he spoke, his voice was as commanding and deep as a medieval king's. "You deserve to feel alive again, *cara*." He ran his hand down the valley between her breasts to rest on her belly. "To feel like the desirable woman you are."

He lowered his head to kiss her cheek. The crook of her neck. Raising her chin, he lowered his lips to her own.

Lucy didn't want to resist. She couldn't fight both him and herself…

She *had* to!

Give herself to a playboy who was incapable of love?

Give herself to a vengeful brute who planned to divorce her before her grandfather was cold in his grave?

"No," she cried, wrenching away. "I—*can't*!"

He looked into her face. Flickers of firelight gleamed in his expressive eyes.

Slowly he gave her a single nod.

"*Bene, cara.* One night. I give it to you as a gift. One night to grieve what you've lost." He turned to face the other side of the bed. "Tomorrow, we start anew. In Rome."

"Rome?" Her teeth chattered with relief. "What's in Rome?"

"Your revenge," he said. "Against Alexander Wentworth."

CHAPTER TEN

HEART in her throat, Lucy turned to Maximo as he slid in next to her in the backseat of the silver Maserati Quattroporte the next morning.

"I can't make Alexander sign this." She shook the legal documents that would terminate his parental rights forever, then stuffed them angrily into her sleek alligator satchel. "I'm telling you right now. Once I show him Chloe's picture, he'll come to his senses and demand to be her father."

"I'm just glad you let me dissuade you from actually bringing the baby, so he won't reject her to her face."

"He won't reject her!" Lucy leaned forward to wave goodbye one last time at Chloe, who was watching from Amelia's arms in an upstairs window. The girl had eagerly volunteered to babysit for a few hours, and the whole household staff was available for any necessary help. Lucy still felt uneasy leaving her baby, but she'd realized it was for the best.

"You act like you still love him."

Maximo's abrupt tone made her sit up straight in her

seat as their chauffeur drove the Maserati smoothly through the villa's gate. "Of course I don't love him!"

"Then why do you persist in believing he'd be a decent father?"

"He's the only father she has." She looked out unhappily through her window at the clear, bright morning. "I can't send him away."

Maximo's cell phone rang. He answered it, speaking in rapid-fire Italian.

She sat next to him on the beige leather seat of the Quattroporte, feeling the hard heat of his leg pressing against hers. She'd spent the whole night quivering on the far side of their bed, unable to sleep. Listening to him breathe next to her. Wanting to be closer. Wanting the comfort of his arms around her. But knowing that would be the most dangerous thing of all.

She hadn't slept a wink. The bags beneath her eyes were roomy enough for international travel.

But obviously he hadn't had the same problem sleeping next to her last night. In his gray wool coat, with his crisp pin-striped suit and clean-shaven jaw, he looked every inch the handsome playboy prince. The kind of man who could take women—and leave them.

Swallowing, Lucy looked away.

As they traveled through Aquillina, she again saw the ramshackle, ruined villa. While the rest of the snow-swept village sparkled like white diamonds in the sun, this solitary place seemed to hunker in shadow.

Then, from the shadows…something *moved*.

Her eyes went wide as she saw an aged, graying old man wearing only an old robe stumble through the doorway. Crying after them, shouting in Italian, he frantically waved his hands.

Lucy twisted her body to stare after him through the back window.

"Stop!" she cried out, reaching forward to grab the driver's shoulder. "Please stop!"

The chauffeur glanced back at Maximo. Hardly pausing in his cell phone conversation, the prince shook his head in refusal.

"Mi scusi, principessa," the driver said apologetically. The sedan continued rapidly down the road.

Lucy glanced through the back window. The old man stood in the middle of the street, staring after them. When they didn't stop, he covered his face with his hands in a gesture of despair.

Furious, she whirled back around in the plush leather seat as Maximo snapped his phone shut.

"Didn't you see that old man calling after you?" she demanded.

"He wasn't calling after me," he replied in a tone of utter boredom. He pulled his laptop computer out of a black leather briefcase. "It's you he wants."

"Me?" she gasped, and instinctively craned her head back around, but they'd already left him far behind. "Why?"

"That man, *cara*," he drawled, "is your sainted grandfather."

"My—grandfather?" she gasped. "And you left him like that in the street? Are you out of your mind?" She turned to the driver. "Stop!" she cried, but the driver kept going. Desperately she grabbed Maximo's arm. "Make him stop! We have to go back! Didn't you see how he needs help?"

Maximo looked at her.

"I would chop off my own hands," he said evenly, "before I'd lift one finger to help that man."

Shocked by the grim, deadly look in his face, she fell back into her seat.

"How can you be so cold?" she whispered. She thought of the old man sobbing in the street. "He's sick and old—dying—"

"A pity he's taking such a long time about it," her husband said coolly.

She gasped. "Don't you have any human feeling at all?"

"No," he said. "Giuseppe Ferrazzi took that from me twenty years ago."

She was frightened by the look in his eyes.

"What—what did he do?"

Maximo's hands tightened. "He destroyed my family. He—"

"What?"

"It doesn't matter. But for every hour he has left on this earth, he will feel the consequence of his actions. I've taken his beloved company. His family. Everything."

She bit her lip. What could her grandfather have done? Surely that poor old man couldn't have destroyed Maximo's family. It all had to be some horrible misunderstanding...

A grandfather. She had a *grandfather*. A wave of protectiveness went through her. "You can't expect me to just let him die!"

He ground his teeth. "I *expect* you to abide by the terms of our agreement. What part of 'honor and obey' don't you understand?"

She muttered, "The same part of 'love' that you don't."

"This is nonnegotiable, Lucia. I have already made it clear to you. Disobey me in this—contact Giuseppe Ferrazzi in any way—and our marriage will end."

She swallowed. She'd lose everything. Her daughter's security—her future.

How could she risk her daughter's well-being for the sake of a dying old man she'd never met?

And yet…how could she live in the same Italian village, knowing he was suffering in poverty, alone and unloved?

"He's my grandfather," she whispered, turning away to stare blindly out at the passing landscape.

There was a long pause.

"We'll be in Rome shortly," Maximo said. "You should think of that. And Wentworth. Do you know why he left you?"

She blinked hard, wiping the tears from her eyes. "His note said he was in love with someone else."

He gave her a sardonic smile. "That's one way to look at it, I suppose. He had a better offer. A former lover suddenly wanted him back, his boss, Violetta Andiemo."

"The fashion designer?" she gasped.

"He wanted the wealth and luxury that she could offer. So when Violetta demanded to know if he'd had any other lovers during their yearlong break, he lied. He said no, that he'd spent the whole time pining for her."

"He said he'd had no other lover?" she whispered.

Alex had kept their daughter a secret—as if Chloe's existence shamed him?

"Violetta Andiemo is forty-five, with all the insecurity and jealousy that comes with an artistic temperament. If she discovers that Wentworth lied—that he took a beautiful young girl as his lover and had a child with her—she'd not only end their engagement, she'd make sure he never got another job. I think that's why he tried to make a secret deal with your grandfather." He shrugged. "They're not even married yet, but I think already he's finding when you marry for money, you earn every cent."

"Tell me about it," she muttered. The car abruptly stopped, and she looked up. Following Maximo's gaze, she saw a helicopter waiting on the tarmac of a small private airport. "What's that?"

"A Sikorsky S-76C," he said, climbing out of the car. Opening her door, he held out his hand. "Our ride."

"A helicopter?" Her voice came out a nervous squeak. "Can't we just drive to Rome?"

"Don't be afraid." His blue eyes smiled down at her. "I think you'll like it."

Like it? That was overstating the case.

As luxurious as the helicopter was, with its white leather seats, flat-screen television and minibar full of champagne, Lucy was relieved to finally descend through the rain clouds that hung thickly gray over Rome. As she and Maximo got into the limo waiting for them on the airport tarmac, her legs still shook from the helicopter's vibrations. It took ten minutes for her ears to stop ringing.

"I got you something," Maximo said as a chauffeur drove them into the center of the rainy, windswept city. He took out a small lavender box from his coat and handed it to her.

Frowning, she opened it.

And was nearly blinded.

Inside the lavender box, nestled in black velvet, was a necklace. She stared at it, only dimly hearing the heavy raindrops pounding the roof of the limo. Hundreds of enormous diamonds sparkled at her.

"Those—those can't be real," she stammered. She looked up at him with pleading eyes. "Tell me those aren't real."

Maximo smiled. "The necklace once belonged to a princess of Hanover. Now it is yours."

All those carats, and it had an exotic history, too? This necklace had to be worth more money than she'd earned in her lifetime!

Was he trying to buy her?

She closed the box with a snap and put it down on the seat between them.

"If you think that this necklace will convince me to take Alex's parental rights away, it won't."

His dark eyebrows lowered, as dark as the clouds outside.

"It is a gift," he said evenly. "Something for you to wear to our wedding."

"Our—wedding?" she gasped. "I thought we were already married!"

"We are." He took her hand in his own, looking at the plain gold band on her finger. "But our marriage must appear real in every way. And you deserve something better than this. You deserve a diamond ring fit for my princess—my bride."

"Oh." Her cheeks flamed red as she tugged on her hand, desperate to get away from his enclosing grasp, to be free of the rush of sensation and confusion it always caused her. "That's all right. Really—"

"No. It is not." Holding firmly to her hand, he brought it to his lips. Gently he kissed each knuckle of her hand. His tongue flicked briefly between her fingers. She froze, unable to move, unable to breathe as she watched him, shockingly imagining his tongue spreading more than her fingers…

"We will have our wedding, *cara*," he murmured. "And afterward, a wedding night."

A wedding night? So he wasn't going to follow through with the threat to seduce her tonight?

She exhaled in relief.

"It will take weeks and weeks to plan a wedding," she said hopefully.

He gave her a wicked grin, as if he knew exactly what she was thinking. "Less than a week, actually. But do not fear." He opened her palm, kissing the tender hollow of her hand. "I won't make you wait that long. Tonight, *cara*. Tonight you will be mine."

He leaned toward her, stroking her hair, and her lips involuntarily parted as she looked into his handsome, arrogant face. If he tried to kiss her now, in the backseat of this Rolls-Royce driving through the wet streets of Rome, could she stop him? Would she have the strength?

"I know it was never your dream to be married in

a hotel," he said. "My men found the book, Lucia. Your dream book. The white church. White dress. Flowers and cake."

They'd found the little book of pictures she'd pulled out from bridal magazines, back when she thought she would be Mrs. Alex Wentworth? Feeling utterly humiliated, she stared blindly at the passing traffic. "That was a long time ago," she said stonily. "Nothing but a girlish dream. Forget it. I have."

"No." Gently he forced her to look at him. "I do not want you to forget. I want you to have it. I want you to have everything you desire."

His words made a tremble go through her soul. How long had she dreamed of a man who would cherish and protect her, and give her the deepest longings of her heart?

He pressed his cheek, already growing rough since he'd shaved that morning, against her own.

"Next week," he murmured against her skin, "we will be wed in the ancient chapel of my villa. Guests have been invited from all over the world. Your wedding planner will arrive on Tuesday from London. You will direct her in your wishes and spare no expense." Pulling away, he smiled down at her. "That is my command."

His command? Oh, how she longed to obey…

It's a trick! she told herself desperately. More bribery. Maximo didn't care about the longings of her heart. He only cared about seduction—and revenge.

Lifting her chin, she folded her arms.

"You say you want me to have everything. Gee, thanks. How about a grandfather? How about a father for my child?"

He stared down at her for a moment, then coolly sat back in his seat. "If you think Wentworth will ever give you or Chloe the care and respect you deserve, you're dreaming, Lucia—"

"Call me Lucy!"

"Once he realizes that he's lost his company's bid for Ferrazzi SpA, and his secret payout from Giuseppe along with it, he'll be more determined than ever to hold on to Violetta." His intense gaze focused on her. "Unless he hears about your fortune. Then he'll want you. Then he'll pretend to love you again."

She shook her head decisively. "I would never take him back in a million years."

"I believe you. But I couldn't be sure of that before," he said quietly. "That's why I had to marry you before he had the chance."

For some reason, his simple words stabbed into her. Maximo had only married her for her trust fund, to make sure that no other man had it. *Of course!* she told herself angrily. How many times did he have to explain it to her?

So why did she keep imagining there was some other reason he'd married her? He claimed to be a cold-hearted, unloving bastard, so why had he been so kind to her? Little things. The birthday party for her daughter. The shopping spree in Milan. The night he'd held her when she'd cried over her mother.

If Maximo had married her just to get revenge on her grandfather, why do all those things?

He'd warned her never to love him. So why was he making it nearly impossible not to? Just to get her into bed?

Maybe. So why did she see something beneath his

eyes when he looked at her? As if she were more precious to him than gold. As if he'd searched for her his whole life…

"Wentworth will try to get you back," he said. "When that doesn't work, he'll try to get custody of Chloe. Either way, he'll try to get your fortune. He would step over you both to get his hands on your money."

"Why are you so scornful?" she whispered, trying desperately to convince herself. "You're using me for your own selfish reasons, just like he did."

Maximo's gaze became as sharp and icy as a blue glacier. "Do not compare us. I'll never pretend to love you, Lucia. I'll never lie to you. But I will always take care of you. You have the prenuptial agreement to prove it."

"Yes. And that's what I don't understand!" She shook her head. "Why have you been so good to me? It's almost enough to make me think…to make me believe…"

That you could love me. But the words were too ridiculous to say aloud. He turned away as his cell phone rang.

"Sì," he responded tersely into the phone, then, *"sì."* He snapped it closed as the limo stopped.

"Wentworth is in there now," Maximo said, pointing at a luxury hotel. "Violetta came from New York just days ago, but they're already quarreling. He's been in the bar for the last hour, drinking as he waits for her to come downstairs."

The hotel's doorman opened the passenger door.

"Go," Maximo said.

She looked back at him. "You're not coming with me?"

He shook his head. "No," he said. "First, I want you

to see the kind of man he truly is. No good as a father. No good to anyone."

"Alex will change his mind when he sees the picture of Chloe," she repeated with more confidence than she felt. "He'll realize he wants to be her father."

He gave her a grim smile. "Try it. Without telling him of your fortune, ask him to be her father. See what happens. The bar is directly to the right off the lobby. Go."

Clutching her handbag to her chest, Lucy stepped out of the limo. The doorman blocked the rain with an umbrella as he escorted her to the main door of the hotel.

Another fancy hotel, she thought dimly, *that will change my life forever.*

Once she was inside the lobby, she turned right and immediately saw him, the man she'd once loved, sitting behind the elegant greenery at the glossy wood bar. He was bouncing his leg nervously, scowling at the doorway.

Then Alex saw her. And the bounce of his leg abruptly stopped.

CHAPTER ELEVEN

"LUCY!" The expressions crossing Alexander's pale face in waves—recognition, shock, horror, anger—would have been comical, if Lucy had been in the mood to laugh. "What are you doing here?"

He looked her over in amazement, from her seven-hundred-dollar ankle boots to her black stockings and cobalt wool shift dress. Her hair was pulled back from her face, showing her chic gold hoops beneath loose dark tendrils that had escaped in the tumult of the helicopter ride. Wearing contacts, her eyes were rimmed with kohl and mascara and her lips were darkened with a classic, subdued shade of autumn wine.

Alex stared at her as if he could barely recognize her. Then his eyes narrowed.

"You should never have come here," he said coldly.

"I had no choice." She held her Ferrazzi satchel closer to her body so he wouldn't see how her hand trembled. Inside the bag, she could see the legal documents that would terminate his parental rights. And next to that—

the photo of Chloe that would finally make him realize that he loved his child. "I have something to show you—"

He stood up from his bar stool. "I don't know how you managed to scrape together enough cash to get to Rome, but you're leaving. Right now."

So he knew how desperately poor she'd been, trying to raise their child. Part of her had hoped he had no idea. That would have made his crime a little less awful. But he'd known all along, and hadn't lifted a finger.

He was really a selfish, shallow bastard...

But he's Chloe's only chance for a father, she told herself desperately. *Any father is better than none.*

Wasn't it?

"Why do you want me to leave, Alex? Are you afraid your fiancée might find out about our baby?"

He grabbed her arm roughly. "For the last time, I'm not that kid's father. Do you understand?"

It was now or never.

With a deep breath, Lucy reached for the photo. It showed Chloe sitting beneath the little tree Lucy had bought for half-price on Christmas Eve just over a week ago. She was holding up her hippo with one hand, a frosted cookie with the other and flashing a big, happy smile that showed nine pearly teeth. The picture showed Chloe's character. Her joy.

"Look." She shoved the picture into his hand.

"What the hell is this—" He started, then stopped.

Lucy held her breath. Her plan was working. Finally, after everything, Alex would realize what a precious gift Chloe was. He would look at her picture and decide to be a decent man—a decent father...

"Her name is Chloe," Lucy blurted out. "She just had her first birthday. She's the sweetest baby, Alex, so smart and loving and fun. But she needs a father. She needs you."

Narrowing his eyes, he slowly looked up at her.

"Christ, what's it going to take to get through to you? I don't want her. And I don't want you."

Opening his hand, he let the photo drop. As if in slow motion, Lucy watched her baby's photo float through the air.

"Now get the hell out of here. I'm with someone new. You and your little brat are nothing to me—"

The picture landed on the floor. She saw her precious baby's photo stepped on by a group of passing businessmen, then scattered beneath the point of a woman's five-inch stiletto.

The woman wearing the stiletto spoke in an icy voice. "Alexander, who is this?"

Alex paled. "Violetta. My darling."

She moved toward them on her viciously sharp heels, and Lucy leaped for her baby's picture. Snatching it from the floor, she cradled it in her hands. Mud had been trodden across her daughter's chubby, smiling face. An eye had been ground into oblivion by Violetta's shoe.

"Answer my question, Alexander." The fashion designer came closer, staring at Lucy with a sneer. Blond and tall, she looked rich, beautiful and miserable. "How do you know this person?"

"I don't," Alex stammered, running his hands nervously through his blond hair. "I just met her."

"I can see how you pass your time when I cannot decide what to wear."

"Honestly, she's a stranger! Nothing to me! I just met her—" he turned to glare at Lucy "—and she was just leaving."

Lucy looked at Alex's handsome, slender face. And she finally understood how he'd been able to propose marriage and beg her to have his baby, then abandon them both. How he'd been able to love her and Chloe one day, then leave them the next.

He didn't care about anyone but himself. He was selfish, lazy and a coward. He'd never understood the joy of real love—or the responsibility that came with it.

Lucy's eyes narrowed.

You don't deserve my baby.

"Yes, I'll leave." She reached back inside her handbag. "As soon as you sign this."

He snatched the papers from her hands. He'd barely skimmed the document for five seconds before his face relaxed. He snapped his fingers at the bartender. "Get me a pen."

The Roman bartender looked down his nose at him with a sigh. *"Sì, signore."*

Alex quickly signed the paper, giving up his rights to Chloe—their beautiful, happy, loving baby—with an enthusiastic flourish. Lucy watched him, feeling sick.

Suddenly she felt a strong, supportive hand on the small of her back. She looked back with an intake of breath.

Maximo's eyes smiled down at her. Giving her comfort. Giving her strength.

Not bothering to even look at her, Alex shoved the paper toward Lucy. "Thanks."

"No, Wentworth," Maximo said. "Thank you."

Alex whirled around as Maximo leaned over the bar to speak to the bartender in Italian. With a glance at Alex, the man nodded and signed.

"D'Aquilla," Alexander said, looking shaken. "What are you doing here?" He tried to smile. "Shouldn't you be on your honeymoon? I heard you married some woman claiming to be the Ferrazzi heiress. Your first mistake, because I'm telling you, we won't let it stand in court. You must be truly desperate if you think you can pull something like…"

His voice trailed off when he saw Maximo's hand on Lucy's back, saw the way she was instinctively leaning toward him for strength.

"What's going on here?" he said faintly.

Maximo turned to him. Looking from one man to the other, Lucy wondered how she could ever have been attracted to Alex. He was blond, slender, washed-out—nothing but a selfish *boy* compared to Maximo. Her dark, fierce husband towered over him in every way possible.

"You're right for once, Wentworth," Maximo said. "I *am* on my honeymoon."

He gave a weak laugh. "I don't get the joke."

"It's no joke." Maximo showed a glint of teeth. "You've lost. Ferrazzi is mine."

"What are you talking about?" Violetta demanded. She turned to Alex. "You said there was no way we could lose. You said you had an inside man."

"He did have an inside man, *signora*," Maximo said.

"Himself. As vice president of acquisitions, he made a deal with Giuseppe Ferrazzi to embezzle millions from your company. So I am sure he is very, very sorry to lose."

She turned on him in fury, thundering, "Alexander!"

Alex ignored her, staring with shock between Lucy and Maximo. "She's your—wife?" he gasped. "That can't be. She's no Ferrazzi!"

"The long-lost Lucia Ferrazzi." Maximo's smile widened into a hard grin. "So much for having her declared dead. Quite the trick of fate. You could have had her for the taking—and the enormous fortune that comes with her."

Alex leaped to his feet with an impassioned gasp.

"Luce. This is all a mistake. I love you. You know I do. And our little baby. You wouldn't take Callie from me—"

Callie?

Maximo had been right all along, down to the last detail. Lucy closed her eyes, feeling like she was going to faint. "Get me out of here," she whispered.

Her husband held her close. For a moment, Lucy leaned against him, accepting his comfort, grateful beyond measure for his protection.

"What do you mean, you love her?" Violetta screeched at Alex. "*You have a baby?* You said you'd been celibate the year we were apart—you swore you loved only me!"

"Shut up!" Alex thundered. "I'm not talking to you!" He turned back to Lucy with pleading brown eyes. "Forgive me. Please, Luce. Take me back. I love you!"

"You're a pathetic excuse for a father, Wentworth,"

Maximo bit out. "A pathetic excuse for a *man*." Taking the paper from the bartender, he tucked it beneath his coat. "Come, *cara*," he said, looking down at her. "We have an appointment with the lawyers."

"No!" Alex's voice hit a higher, more furious pitch with every word. "No! Damn it—where's that paper? Callie is my daughter—I deserve half—that document won't hold up in court. It wasn't witnessed!"

His voice ended in a gurgle as Violetta threw his drink into his face.

"*Sì*, it was." Maximo gave a pleasant nod to the enraged fashion designer. "*Signora*, enjoy your evening."

And gathering up Lucy, who was still numb with shock and grief, he led her away from Alex's furious screams and out into the endless rain of the Eternal City.

Two hours later, as she left the judge's office in Rome, the screams of Alex's lawyers were still ringing in her ears. They'd been at first suspicious, then furious, to find their attempt to declare her dead a failure at the very moment they'd expected victory. Unable to buy her trust fund shares from Giuseppe Ferrazzi, they were forced to accept that Maximo now owned seventy percent of the company, making their own thirty percent a useless afterthought.

"It's done, *cara*," Maximo said as they went downstairs to the waiting limo. "We've won. Wentworth has lost his lover—and his job. Ferrazzi is mine."

Yes, she thought numbly. They'd won. Her grandfather was dying alone in a dark, ruined villa. Her precious baby had just lost her only father. Some victory!

But Maximo didn't seem to feel that way. The expression on his face was triumphant. His smile was glinty and cruel.

He was *reveling* in his revenge.

It made her suck in her breath. How could he be so good to her—and so vicious to a poor old man?

Who was Prince Maximo d'Aquilla? Did she really know him at all—any more than she'd truly known Connie Abbott, or Alex?

Nothing made sense anymore. Her body felt numb, and her mind still didn't seem to be working properly. At the hotel bar, facing Alex, she'd clung to Maximo. For one moment, she'd felt like she could trust him, felt it down to her bones. She'd believed her husband was an oasis of honor and strength in the cold, selfish world.

But it had only been an illusion. *Again.*

She kept trying to see good in him—good that wasn't there. She stumbled. What was wrong with her?

Catching her, Maximo took her by the elbow, escorting her into the waiting Rolls-Royce. "Are you all right, *cara*?"

She didn't answer.

"Lucia?" Maximo said, sitting next to her in the back seat as the car sped away from the curb. "It is better that Wentworth no longer has a claim on your daughter. Surely you are glad to know the truth?"

"I don't know anymore," she muttered, crossing her arms tightly over her chest. She turned her head toward the windows, staring out at the rain.

"Once their DNA test is completed, they will have

no choice but to accept your identity, and the Ferrazzi company will be ours."

"You mean yours."

"*Sì.*" His voice was matter-of-fact. "Is that why you are upset? You do not wish me to control it?"

"I wish you to forgive my grandfather," she said, her voice breaking. "He's my family."

His jaw hardened. "Chloe is your only real family."

"And she no longer has a father."

"Better no father at all than a man like Wentworth."

"But now…" She took a deep breath. "We're both alone."

"No."

His blue eyes caught hers, wouldn't let them go.

"You won't be alone for long. You are a woman who was made for love. You should have a family, Lucia. A faithful, loving husband, a houseful of children. I want all those things for you."

The images battered her like wind in a storm.

The happy home. The children. And a husband who adored her.

If Maximo could give her those things…

"Is that what you want?" she whispered.

"*Sì, cara,* it is." He paused, and for one minute she could barely breathe. Then he continued, "I want those things for you. After we are divorced, I will introduce you to friends—good men, not fortune hunters—who desire a wife."

"But not you."

He looked at her. "Between us it is only business, *cara.* You know this. Business and pleasure. I am not a man to settle down. Love only complicates what should be simple. But not all men think so. I have a friend in Rio, a self-made billionaire who might—"

"No, thanks." Her voice cracked as she turned back to face the window. Just when she'd almost convinced herself he might care for her, he was already plotting to pawn her off on some Brazilian stranger. "I'm happy alone. Chloe can do without a father. I don't need a loving husband or a houseful of children. Just Chloe and me and our thirty million dollars. Perfect."

Telling all these lies, her vision grew blurry.

She covered her face. "I've never been so *happy*."

She heard the soft click as he undid his seat belt. Then she felt his hands unclicking hers. A moment later, he pulled her into his arms, wrapping himself around her. She felt all his warmth and comfort. The hard, jagged lump in her throat—the one she'd felt ever since Alex had dropped her baby's photo like trash—dissolved, and she began to sob.

Maximo held her closer, stroking her hair. He murmured soft words in Italian that she couldn't understand, but for some reason his kindness only made her cry harder.

"Why are you treating me like this?" she choked out. "I don't understand. You could have offered me a small financial settlement for my shares. Instead you insisted on giving me thirty million. You could have married me and left me in Chicago. Instead you brought me to your villa and made me a princess. Why?"

"I told you. I want the old man to die knowing that everything he's ever cared about is mine."

She shook her head. "It's more than that," she whispered. "If it weren't, you would ignore me when we're alone. Instead, even in private, you treat me like your princess. You try to fulfill my every dream."

His jaw clenched as he looked away. "You are giving me too much credit."

"No, I'm not." Tears were streaming unchecked down her face. "We're practically strangers, but ever since we met you've acted like—"

Like you love me, she almost said, but she didn't have the nerve. Especially since she knew it wasn't true. He had said it a hundred times: he would never love her.

But how was she supposed to believe that, when his actions spoke so differently?

"Perhaps," he said, stroking her cheek, "it is all to lure you into my bed."

Could it be? She closed her eyes, savoring his touch. She was married to a handsome prince. She was wealthy beyond belief. Her daughter was happy and well cared for. She had everything she'd ever wanted. She was living in a fairy tale.

So why was she so miserable?

Because there was one thing she didn't have. Love. The handsome prince didn't love her. They would divorce in a matter of months, and he would move on to the next gorgeous woman who took his fancy. Chloe would grow up without a father. And Lucy would live forever in some luxurious villa, a princess in diamonds—alone.

She pulled away.

"Please," she whispered, covering her face with her hands, "just take me back to my daughter."

She felt him staring down at her.

"Basta," he suddenly muttered. "Enough of this."

Enough? She looked up. Just like that, he was done? He was so powerful that he could simply decide not to feel things like love or grief?

She wished she could do the same.

Maximo leaned forward to speak in Italian to the chauffeur. When he sat back next to her, he said, "You need heat and sunshine, *cara*, the kind that will make you warm again. You need the wind against your face, the smell of flowers waving in the fields. You and your baby need light and air. But you also—" he reached over to her, stroking the bare skin of her collarbone "—need to feel young again. To remember that you are young and beautiful."

Young and beautiful? She shuddered as his smooth stroke sent waves of pleasure down her breasts. How could she ever feel young ever again?

"I'm taking you on a vacation," he said firmly.

"A vacation?" She hiccuped a giddy laugh. "That's good. Because I was getting so tired—" she waved her hand around the backseat of the Rolls-Royce limousine "—of putting up with all *this*."

He gave her a crooked grin. "Then you will enjoy our trip very much."

She licked her lips. "So what are you thinking? Meeting up with your friends at a private Caribbean island? Sailing the Greek islands on your yacht?" She shook her head. "I'm not used to it, Maximo. Being watched by servants. Surrounded by your friends—" *by your ex-mistresses* "—who can't understand why you married me."

"You're out of your mind if you think I'm going to invite any of them on my honeymoon."

She stared at him.

"Honeymoon?" she croaked.

"Sì." He looked down at her. His eyes were darkly blue. Sensual. Arrogant. "Did you think I'd forgotten my promise? No, *cara*. For too long, I have held myself back. Given you time to grieve." He stroked her cheek with a predatory smile. "But my patience is over."

She nearly gasped as he stroked down her neck, resting his hand between her breasts.

"Tonight, *cara*, I will show you how good pleasure can feel. I will take you to bed. I will at last make you mine." He leaned forward, his eyes a challenge as he whispered, "Just try to resist me."

CHAPTER TWELVE

THEY arrived at a private airport in southern Sicily shortly before sunset.

Lucy descended from the plane with Chloe in her arms. It was so warm, she'd left her coat in her suitcase, and now wore only a white cotton blouse, slim dark jeans and wedge sandals. Her dark hair, tied back with a green silk headband, was whipped by a warm breeze as she came down the steps to the tarmac. The wind was fragrant with flowers and the salty tang of the sea. Above their heads, palm trees swayed.

Ahhhh...*Sicily*. She took a deep breath, and suddenly, the weight on her shoulders seemed to lighten. Though it was January, she'd at last seen the warm Italy of her dreams.

But at the bottom of the steps, she stopped. She didn't see a Rolls-Royce or anything remotely like a limo. In fact, the only car parked anywhere on the pavement of the tiny private airport was a beat-up old truck. Confused, she looked to the right and left. "Where's our car?"

Pulling their luggage from the plane himself, he nodded toward the old truck. "Right there."

"That? It doesn't even have a roof!"

"It's a convertible. A classic." He tossed their luggage in the back of the truck. He'd rolled back his sleeves, the first time she'd ever seen him do so, and her eyes unwillingly traced his muscular forearms, lightly dusted with dark hair. "Lucy?"

She abruptly focused on his face. "Yes?"

Slowly his lips spread into an arrogant, knowing grin. "Do you like it?"

Blushing that he'd caught her, she shook her head emphatically and pointed quickly at the truck. "If you like antiques, you should have kept my old Honda."

He gave a mock sigh. "A pity we donated that to charity." He tossed a long, lean leg over the driver's-side door. She couldn't help but gawk at his muscular backside. She'd never seen him wear jeans before.

"Need some help getting Chloe into the back?"

He'd caught her again!

"No. I can do it." Cheeks flaming, she hurried to put her daughter into the baby seat snugly beneath the roll bar in the back. She snapped her five-point buckle, then climbed in next to Maximo.

He gunned the engine, driving from the airport along a rough gravel road. She could see the blue water of the sea sparkling beneath the cliffs, see palm trees swaying in the warm breeze. Leaning back, she felt the Mediterranean sun on her face. Her hair blew in every direction in the roofless truck, and it felt like spring. Glancing at Maximo, she actually smiled.

Before she remembered and her whole body became tense again.

Tonight.

He planned to seduce her tonight.

And she would resist. *She had to.* She could not give in to her desire. No matter how wonderfully he treated her or how easily his kisses could seduce her. She didn't care what he said. If she gave him her body, her heart would soon follow. All her defenses would fall like dominoes.

She'd fall in love with him, just like all the other foolish women.

In spite of knowing he was a coldhearted, vengeful playboy who planned to divorce her as soon as her grandfather was dead. In spite of the fact that he'd outright told her that if she chose to love him, he would break her heart.

Had she learned absolutely nothing from her last mistake of loving someone?

"You're looking at me again," he said. "What are you thinking?"

"I'm thinking you should forgive my grandfather. I'm sure whatever he did was an accident, or a misunderstanding. I'm sure he would never hurt anyone."

"Always believing the best of people," he said quietly. "You don't know him, Lucy."

"But—"

"No."

They rode several miles in silence.

She suddenly looked at him. "You called me Lucy. Not Lucia."

He shrugged.

"Why?"

"Because it's what you prefer."

It infuriated her how much that small concession pleased her. Why did she care? It was a meaningless gesture. Part of his seduction.

Pushing her wildly waving hair out of her eyes, she gave him an attempt at a smile. "I've never seen you like this before. Wearing jeans. Driving your own car."

He gave her a sidelong glance. "I'm on my honeymoon."

And he'd made his intentions all too clear. She shivered in the warm sun.

As the last burst of red sun began to fade behind the horizon, he turned down a dusty road past a grove of olive trees. At the end of the road, a little stone cottage sat on the edge of the sea cliff, surrounded by beeches and irrigated roses in bloom. Light shone from every window.

"This is our hotel?"

"It's not a hotel," he said briefly. "I grew up here."

"I thought you grew up in Aquillina."

"Only until I was twelve. After my parents and sister died, my aunt gave up her *penzione* and moved Amelia and me back here, closer to her husband's family."

Lucy straightened in surprise. He'd mentioned before that he had no family, but she hadn't known...hadn't realized...

"Your parents and sister died? I'm so sorry." She paused, biting her lip. "What happened?" She paused in sudden fear. "My grandfather had nothing to do with it, did he?"

Stopping the truck, he pulled the parking brake. He

got out of the truck, pulling their luggage out of the back and hefting it over his back. "It's getting late. I want to start cooking dinner before Chloe is too tired to eat."

"You!" she gasped. "Cook dinner?"

"You said you didn't want any servants. So I'm what you get." His face was half concealed by shadow. "But I can still have my yacht brought from Antibes if you prefer. We'd have a staff of twenty and a full-time nanny. We could sail to the Costa Smeralda, Tunisia, Cairo. Anywhere you like. Just say the word."

She bit her lip.

Opt for the yacht, the voice of caution whispered.

Because this snug little rose cottage by the sea was dangerous. It was everything she'd once dreamed of. All it needed was a happy family inside and it would be perfect.

This cottage tempted her to remember her lost illusions.

But even knowing this, she couldn't resist the bright windows drawing her in from the twilight…

"Who left the lights on?" Lucy asked as she walked through the cottage with Chloe yawning in her arms. Though spare in decoration and very rustic, the house was cozy. A fire blazed in the old stone fireplace. "Who started the fire for us?"

"My aunt. She lives over the hill." He put the suitcases down by the bedroom doors. "She wouldn't leave Sicily, even when I offered her the Villa Uccello. So I bought all the adjoining land here instead and built her a *palazzo*. She has servants of her own now, but still

likes to welcome me back when I come for a visit." He
gave a brief smile. "Old habits die hard, I suppose."

"All your women must love this house," she said
wistfully.

"My women?"

"Yes." She swallowed. "All the women you bring
here."

"I have never brought a mistress here," he said, then
looked at her. "Just you."

She was the first woman he'd ever brought home?

Don't be seduced, she pleaded with herself. *Don't be
seduced into thinking you're special to him!*

But it still made her shiver. As he cooked them a
simple dinner of pasta and steamed broccoli, with a
bottle of milk for Chloe and a bottle of red wine from
the nearby D'Aquilla vineyards for Lucy and Maximo,
the air seemed to thicken and hum with sexual tension.

Lucy drank a glass of wine…then another…then
another. She drank and ate slowly, trying to prolong the
meal as long as possible. By the glint in his eyes, she knew
that as soon as dinner was over and the baby was asleep,
he intended to make good on his promise of seduction.

But finally, Chloe was yawning and literally falling
asleep in the old wooden high chair, and Lucy had no
choice but to put her to bed. She gave Chloe a quick
bath, dried her with the thick cotton towel, then dressed
her in soft new pajamas. For an instant, she held her
close, savoring her clean baby smell.

As Maximo knelt at the stone fireplace, stoking the
fire to stave off the night's chill, Lucy carried her
droopy-eyed child to the small bedroom. Lucy kissed

her baby good-night, tucking her into the crib with a warm blanket.

Then, leaning against the door, she took a deep breath and practiced what she would say.

Maximo, I can't let you seduce me.

I'm not like you. I can't keep my heart out of it.

Our three-month marriage must be in name only.

She clenched her hands into fists, drumming up her strength. She would be firm. She would resist.

But as soon as she left the room, she saw Maximo standing in front of the fire, his blue eyes dark with need. She'd barely closed Chloe's bedroom door before he started for her. His powerful body moved toward her like a predator, his handsome face half in shadow.

She swallowed. "Maximo," she said, "I won't—"

But that was as far as she got before he pulled her against his body. His arms held her tight.

And he ruthlessly kissed her.

He pressed her mouth wide, bruising her lips. He tantalized her with his tongue, convincing her with an argument all his own. He held her hips possessively, stroking her backside as her full, aching breasts were crushed against his chest; and her protests turned to a sigh as she was enfolded and utterly consumed by his kiss.

"Lucy," he whispered against her skin. "Lucy, *ti desidero. Sei bellissima…*"

She felt his hands on her waist beneath her blouse. Slowly his touch moved up her skin, causing a heat to spread up and down her body that had nothing to do with the fire.

Gently he picked her up and carried her to the sofa in front of the old stone fireplace. She shivered as he stepped back from her, standing in a beam of moonlight. Outside, a fierce January wind rattled the windowpanes.

In here, they were safe. In here, no one could touch her. *Except him.*

With his gaze fixed on hers, he pulled off his shirt. She nearly gasped at the hard planes of his muscular chest, revealed in the moonlight and flickering shadows of the fire. Dark hair dusted from his tiny nipples to his flat, taut belly, disappearing beneath his waistband.

She swallowed, barely able to breathe.

He lowered himself over her on the sofa. As he kissed her, she could already feel herself surrendering.

He unbuttoned her shirt, and she made no resistance. His fingertips traced the lace of her bra. Her breasts felt so taut, her nipples so hard, that she held her breath as he undid the clasp. He reached beneath the fabric and cupped her breasts with his hands. Sparks shot down her body. As he lowered his mouth to one nipple, stroking the other between his fingers, she almost cried out...

She'd never felt like this before.

She wanted him. All of him.

She wanted him to rip off her clothes and bury himself in her. She wanted to scream and sigh and pound and *love*...

"No!"

It took all her force of will to push him away with a hard shove to his chest. Their eyes locked. "I can't do this," she panted. "However easy it is for you, it will make me...emotionally involved."

"We already are emotionally involved, *cara.*"

Her heart stopped. "We are?"

"Of course." He gave her a smooth Italian smile. "You are my wife. For the next few months, I will fulfill your every wish. And—" his lips spread in a wicked smile "—I'll satisfy your every desire…"

She swallowed. She wanted him—but she couldn't have him. She already felt close, too close, to tipping over: from merely caring for him to far more…

"I can't!" Her frustrated body made emotion spill out of her like tears. "Don't you understand what this does to me?"

"Let's play a game," he said, running his fingers along her naked belly in the moonlight.

"A game?"

"*Sì.*"

It sounded innocent enough. Anything had to be better than being lured back into the unimaginable, soul-stealing pleasure of his kiss. "What is the game?"

His eyes met hers. "I try to make you explode with pleasure. You try to resist."

A cloud passed over the moon outside, and for a moment, she could see only the dark silhouette of his face, hear only the furious pounding of her heart.

She whispered, "And if I resist you?"

"I will accept your demand for a marriage in name only." He stroked up her belly beneath her shirt. Taking her hand, he lightly kissed the palm, then placed it against his naked, muscular chest "But if I make you moan and shiver and gasp in my arms, you are completely mine for the next three months."

By the look on his face, he did not expect to lose.

"How long would the game last?" His "game" wasn't so different from the battle she'd already been fighting since the day they'd met.

"Twenty-four hours."

A whole day and night? Was he kidding? She stared at him, wide-eyed.

"Starting now." He stood up, holding his hand out to help her up. "Those are my terms. Do you agree?"

She stared at his outstretched hand. Endure this assault of sensual pleasure for twenty-four hours without giving in? Impossible!

And yet, the prize glittered before her: She'd be able to survive the next three months without surrendering either body or soul. Being married to Maximo was hard enough. She could see why so many women fell for him. But she couldn't allow herself to do the same. Otherwise, when he abandoned her when her grandfather died, she would be devastated. Crushed. She'd be no good to Chloe. No good to anyone. And she would have only herself to blame for not being strong enough to resist the playboy prince.

Twenty-four hours. Could she do it?

She had no choice, she realized. What was the alternative? Twenty-four hours—or simply wait for him to seduce her at will during the next few months, anytime, anywhere?

This was her only chance at survival. Holding her breath, she put her hand in his.

"I accept."

He pulled her up from the sofa. Her body pressed

against his, her naked breasts against his hard, dark-haired chest.

"Bene," he whispered, stroking her cheek. He lowered his mouth to hers.

His kiss made her ache from within. She felt his hands everywhere: cupping her breasts, clasping her backside, stroking the inside of her thighs over her jeans. Gently he laid her back against the sofa, pressing his heavy body against her own. She could feel his hardness against her, and it was sweet agony as he slowly ravaged her resolve with exquisite, practiced touches that showed her why no woman on earth could resist him.

I can handle this, she told herself desperately. *I can.*

But her whole body was exploding with bliss and longing. She felt as soft and yielding as honey. With his every kiss, she lost her mind; with his every touch, she found it harder and harder to remember why she'd forbidden herself to surrender.

Gasping out a hoarse breath, she looked desperately at the old clock over the fireplace. Would the torture soon be over? How long had she endured?

Twenty minutes?

She swore aloud as he kissed her, covering her profanity with his sweet, sweet mouth. She fell back against the sofa, pulled beneath his body, drowning in pleasure…

Then, from the small bedroom, Chloe gave a startled little cry. She sometimes woke at night, and nearly always fell back asleep on her own. But Lucy seized on it as a daughter's gift—Chloe unknowingly protecting her mother from her weakness. *Thank you*, she thought gratefully, and pushed away from the couch.

"Where do you think you're going?"

"I agreed to your bargain," she said, buttoning up her shirt. "But you don't expect me to just let my baby cry?"

"Lucy—"

"She's just scared to be sleeping alone in a new place. She's lonely," she said hastily. "I'll see you in the morning." Evading his arms, she ran for the little bedroom, closing the door behind her—and locking it.

She took a deep breath, leaning back against the door. She glanced at the crib. Chloe was already asleep again, but Maximo didn't need to know that.

With a little luck, she thought, hunting through the dark for her suitcase, they would both sleep until late in the morning. Then, she would only have twelve hours to resist Maximo's powerful onslaught—and her own aching need.

Rummaging through the suitcase, Lucy found her pajama top, but couldn't find the pants. Putting on the silk shirt, she climbed into the wire-framed twin bed beside the crib.

Twelve hours?

It would take a miracle for her to win this wretched, horrible, agonizingly sweet war.

CHAPTER THIRTEEN

BANG—crash—bang!

Lucy's eyelids fluttered. For a moment, stretching her body against the soft mattress, she was still in her dream. It had been so wonderful. A happy family living in a rose-covered cottage by the sea. A houseful of children, laughing and playing. And after they were asleep, a dark, handsome prince had taken her to bed at night, making her moan and scream with pleasure such as she'd never known...

Their bargain.

Her eyes flew open. She was in the snug little bedroom, lying on the slender mattress with an old metal frame, beneath a handmade quilt. On the nearby nightstand, she saw a basin full of freshly cut roses.

She sat up. Warm sunlight scattered across the old handwoven rug on the hardwood floor. It was late morning.

"We did it," she whispered aloud. "We slept late. Chloe—"

But the crib was empty!

Crash—bang—crash!

Where was her baby? Lucy leaped out of bed. Wearing nothing more than a silk pajama top that barely reached the tops of her thighs, she pushed open the door and ran out into the hall.

What she saw in the kitchen made her stop in her tracks.

Two pairs of eyes looked up at her. Chloe was sitting on the rug in front of the stove, her chubby fists holding two big wooden spoons, which she was using to beat heartily upon an upside-down copper pot placed in front of her. Blue smudges covered her baby's chin and mouth as Chloe looked up at her with a joyful smile.

And behind the baby, his face dusted with flour and looking adorably out of place, was Maximo. Making breakfast.

"Buon giorno, cara." Setting down a plate of fresh blueberry scones, he pulled her close and kissed first one cheek, then the other. "Would you like some coffee?"

Bemused, she nodded.

"Sit down. Cream? Sugar?"

"Yes," she blurted, sinking into a chair at the kitchen table.

She didn't understand. She'd cheated him of the first twelve hours of their bargain. So where was the payback? Why wasn't he tossing her over his shoulder like a sack of potatoes and carrying her to his bedroom right now?

"Did you sleep well?" He brought her a cup of coffee with cream and sugar. Without even trying to touch her, he turned his back and started packing a picnic basket.

"I…um…yes," she mumbled. She took a bracing sip of coffee.

"Bene." He put some wrapped sandwiches and silverware into the basket. "The weather looks to be very fine today. I thought we'd go for a picnic brunch after you have your coffee. It should be unseasonably hot." He looked her over from her silk pajama top to her bare legs. "Hotter than I've known for a long, long time."

Her body turned to steam under his gaze, even as things suddenly made sense again.

He meant to seduce her on the picnic.

She hastily plotted her defense. She would wear the closest thing to a snowsuit she could find. She would keep her daughter close at all times. If Chloe sneezed, Lucy would claim she had an impending cold; if Chloe whined, Lucy would say she needed a nap. Both good reasons to bring her inside.

Her baby would protect her.

As if on cue, Chloe crawled toward her, then held up her arms. Lucy picked her up and hugged her close. Her baby's chubby cheeks were smeared with blueberries. For a playboy who had no experience with children, Maximo seemed to know just how to delight her baby.

It was a pity Maximo wasn't Chloe's father...

The thought stopped her cold. It was bad enough that Lucy wanted Maximo in her bed. But to also wish he could be her child's father—a man who'd sworn he would never settle down? How stupid could her blind heart be?

Stop it, she told her errant heart. Stop it right now.

"Did you say something, *cara*?"

Dear heaven, had she mumbled the words aloud?

"I was just wondering how long Chloe has been awake?"

"Two hours."

"Two hours?" she gasped. "Why didn't you wake me?"

He shrugged, lifting his hands in an expressive gesture. "I heard her talking in her crib, and I was awake anyway, checking sales figures from our Tokyo office. I thought you might appreciate a lie-in."

It was the first time she'd had the luxury of sleeping in since Chloe had been born. Lucy felt wonderful. Well-rested. But she didn't understand. He'd given up two of the precious twelve hours left—to let her sleep?

"Thank you. But your gallantry will not help you win." The extra sleep had only made her stronger for battle. "You've just made your first mistake."

"We'll see." He allowed himself a private smile. "If you are done with your coffee, shall we get ready to go?"

Chloe gurgled nonsense syllables at him, waving her wooden spoon happily.

"What's that you say?" He warmly smiled down at the baby. "You want us to hurry?"

Lucy laughed up at them, then stopped.

Realization ripped through her like the beam of sunlight through the mullioned windows.

This. This was the family life she'd always dreamed of. This moment, right here. A laughing child, a warm kitchen, a handsome husband.

This was happiness…

It's an illusion! she told herself desperately.

But her feelings only intensified as the three of them shared a picnic, sitting on a blanket on a hillside of flowers overlooking the sea. They laughed and ate a simple repast of roast beef sandwiches and fruit, with blueberry scones for dessert.

Afterward, in the sun-drenched field of flowers, beneath the wide blue Sicilian sky, Lucy actually saw her daughter take her first steps.

Three trembling, falling baby steps from Maximo's arms to hers. And Lucy was here to see her daughter's milestone. Thanks to Maximo.

"Thank you," she whispered, looking up at his handsome face with a kind of dazed joy. "Thank you for making it possible for me to be with her."

He held Chloe's hands as she stood unsteadily on her feet. Reaching for the petals of a flower, the baby lost her balance and plopped back on the blanket. She spotted the picnic basket, crawled to it and discovered the last scone with a delighted cackle.

"I'm happy to be here with you. Both of you," Maximo said. Something in the tone of his voice made Lucy turn to look at him. His eyes were an endless deep blue. "If I were the sort of man who wanted to settle down, I might think…"

"Think what?" she said, holding her breath.

"Kiss me."

Across the blanket, he moved his head toward her and she couldn't move away. *Just a kiss*, she told herself. Surely nothing bad could come of a single kiss? She'd worn skinny jeans—tight and very hard to take off—and a Victorian-inspired, high-necked blouse with a dozen tiny buttons. With his big fingers, Maximo would never be able to get the shirt off her.

And if that didn't work, there was Chloe sitting next to them. She'd need a bath with all the blueberries she had plastered to her hair and clothes...

"*Salve*, Maximo!" A woman's voice called from a distance behind them.

They both turned. Lucy saw an older woman waving at them as she descended over the hill. She had a chic white pageboy haircut, unlined skin and a happy smile.

"*Salve!*" he called back.

"Who's that?"

"My *zia*—my aunt Silvana." He gave Lucy a grin. "She'll be watching Chloe for the rest of the afternoon. Just in case she gets lonely and needs company."

A flutter of nerves went through her belly. So he'd seen through her baby ploy, had he?

Of course he had. She bit her lip. "That's Amelia's mother? She's beautiful."

"Yes." He stared out toward his aunt. "So beautiful that your grandfather wanted to marry her."

"My grandfather proposed to her?" Lucy said in shock, wondering if she'd heard wrong. "But he's so much older than she is!"

"He was a forty-year-old widower with a son when he moved to Aquillina, and she was fifteen. But he fancied himself desperately in love." He gave a brief, humorless smile. "Of course, my grandfather scorned the offer. Who was Ferrazzi? Nobody. What right did the nouveau riche son of a Roman shopkeeper have to marry a princess d'Aquilla? My grandfather slapped him for even asking. Ferrazzi swore he'd get even for the insult."

He stopped, clenching his jaw.

"And...did he?" Lucy breathed. "Get even?"

Maximo finally looked at her, his eyes as blue as a haunted sea. "*Sì*. Long after my grandfather was dead, long after my aunt was married to another man, Ferrazzi got his revenge on my whole family."

She reached for him. "Maximo—what did he do?"

He just shook his head. "Silvana." He rose to his feet as his aunt came within earshot. "I'm so glad you could come." He picked up the baby, cradling her in his strong, muscular arms. "This is Chloe."

"*Faccia bedda!*" Silvana exclaimed. "What a sweet little face!"

Smiling, she held out her arms, and after a brief moment of hesitation Chloe went to her. The older woman slung the Ferrazzi diaper bag over her other shoulder, then departed with a wave. It all happened so quickly that by the time Lucy reacted, it was too late. They were gone.

"Wait! Where are they going?"

"To my aunt's *palazzo*. She'll bring Chloe back home after dinner."

Scowling, she turned on Maximo angrily. "That's not fair! You distracted me with that story of my grandfather—it was never part of our deal to—"

"Fair?" He gave her a hot glance. "Let me show you fair."

He swept her up in his arms, setting her down on the blanket in the field of flowers. For an instant, she was dazzled by the image of his silhouette against the bright blue sky, the warm Sicilian sun.

"After your trick last night, I wanted to make sure you had no excuses. Nowhere to run. Where will you flee now? You play dirty, *cara*," he growled, "then so do I."

Slowly he popped the buttons from her shirt. Removing her bra, leaving her naked from the waist up beneath the sun, he lowered his head between her breasts.

She gasped as he suckled one taut nipple, then the other. She strained beneath his weight, trying to twist away from his strong hands.

"No—" she whimpered, wanting him desperately. "Please. You can't—"

He silenced her with a kiss. Taking off his black T-shirt, he pulled her onto his lap, facing him. Through the jeans, she could feel how much he wanted her. Against her will, she swayed against him with an intake of breath.

He gave her a wolflike smile.

"And now," he ordered, brushing her hair off her face, "you are going to kiss me."

Sitting in his lap, her legs wrapped around his waist and her blouse ripped open beneath the hot sun, she felt his skin against hers. Her breasts were crushed against his dark-haired chest. His heart against her heart. Her body snug against his. She heard the cry of birds overhead and felt the sun on her face.

And Lucy knew she was going to lose—everything.

CHAPTER FOURTEEN

WIND blew the flowers and grass of the field around them, waving the branches of the olive grove as Maximo looked at her beneath the hot Sicilian sun.

And he knew she was his for the taking.

Her eyes were closed, her lashes dark against her creamy skin. Her head was tilted back to expose her trembling neck. Dark hair tumbled down her shoulders, against the white cotton that barely clung to her arms, against her magnificent breasts, high and full with nipples the color of pale April roses...

He shook his head in amazement. How could he have ever thought Lucy was plain? She was more than a beauty. She was a *goddess*. And she didn't know. Her innocence of her own power intoxicated him.

She was fated to be his.

Maximo never wanted to let her go.

Find her a new husband? *Dio santo.* He must have been out of his mind to even suggest it. Introduce her to his friend in Rio? *Maledizione.* Joaquim would take one look at those long legs, full breasts and gorgeous smile and be only too happy to consider her as his potential bride.

And then Maximo would have to kill him.

With a low growl, he stood up from the blanket. He picked her up, her legs still wrapped around his waist. She clung to him in surprise, her eyelids fluttering in bewilderment.

"What—" she whispered. "Where—"

"I'm taking you home," he said gruffly.

But the way her body felt against him as he carried her, even her slender weight was an unbearable burden. The path along the cliffs, which had been so pleasurable on their walk to the picnic, was now a long journey of unbearable agony. All he wanted to do was satiate his desire for her satin-smooth skin, her tart mouth, the full curve of her backside, the heaven of her breasts. To push her down amid the flowers, rip off her clothes, and push himself into her until they both exploded. To feel her body convulse around him.

But there was something more he wanted. Something he didn't understand. It made every nerve in his body taut with the drive to possess her.

She belonged to him. It was fate. He would allow no other man to touch her—ever.

He barely made it back to the cottage. He went to the master bedroom, tossed her on the bed. He peeled off her snug jeans and panties. He could bear it no more. This taut desire for her was making him *pazzo*, demented. Spreading her legs apart, he buried his head between her thighs and tasted her.

She gasped, arching her back as she grabbed his shoulders.

"Please—" she panted. "Please."

Was she begging him to relent or to continue? He wondered if she herself even knew.

"Don't come, *cara*," he whispered. "Stay still. Resist me. Do not explode with pleasure, and I will let you go."

But it was a lie. He would never let her go now...

He touched her thighs, lightly caressing the hair between her legs. He stroked her with his finger, relishing her slick, satiny wetness. He wanted nothing more than to pull off his jeans and thrust himself inside her, but he forced himself to wait, to delay his own pleasure. Because this was about far more than his own ecstasy.

He wanted to possess her completely, body and soul.

He wanted to hear her admit that she was his.

She cried out as he caressed her with his tongue. Beads of sweat broke out on his forehead from the exquisite pain of holding himself back as she twisted her hips beneath him.

He held her down. Stretching her wide, he lapped her with the full width of his tongue. With agonizing slowness, he pushed one finger inside her, then two. She was so taut, he thought. So ready. He groaned aloud, not sure how much longer he could withstand this torture.

Moving up, he kissed her dark hair, her belly, finally her breasts. He suckled her, squeezing the other breast with his fingers as his palm rubbed against her mound in an erotic circle.

He felt her tense and tremble beneath him...

Leaning forward, he whispered against her ear, "Don't come, Lucy. Don't."

He slowly pushed two fingertips inside her, inch by inch, swirling the nub of her pleasure with his thumb. He heard her suck in her breath. And hold it. Then she started to gasp. He felt her tighten around his fingers. Her whole body shook as her gasp crescendoed into a loud, terrible cry of ecstasy.

For one perfect moment, joy went through him as he closed his eyes in triumph. She was his. He'd never had to try so hard for any woman as he had for his wife.

His wife. At that thought, Maximo, the playboy prince who'd had more women than he could count, nearly lost his self-control like an untried teenager.

Ripping off his jeans, he fell upon her, kissing her neck. Sliding a condom down his painfully hard shaft, he positioned himself between her legs. He could feel her hot wetness, her sweetness, and thought he would die if he didn't—

"Maximo."

He abruptly focused on her face. Tears were coursing down her cheeks.

Dio santo!

"Lucy," he gasped. "You're crying!"

If he'd hurt her—

She shook her head. "You've won." Her voice trembled. "I'm yours forever."

Forever? The word shocked him. It was too perilously close to his own traitorous thoughts. He quickly shook his head. "No, *cara*, no. You've always known that our marriage is just—"

She stopped him by putting a finger against his lips. "I know."

Lucy, his forever? Ridiculous thought! He wanted to satiate himself with her, that was all. A three-month affair. Six months. A year or two at most. And while they were together, they could pretend to be in love. Pretend to be a family. He would have her every night. And if a condom broke, if he accidentally got her pregnant...

Pregnant.

The thought of Lucy pregnant with his child finally made him lose the last of his control.

Taking her finger into his mouth, he sucked it. He kissed up her bare arm to her neck. He lowered his body against hers and kissed her lips. She returned the kiss passionately, no longer trying to fight, and he entwined her tongue with his own. He stroked his hands down her body, caressing her belly, her backside and finally her hips. She swayed against him with a whimper.

"*Sì, cara, sì,*" he said hoarsely. Feeling like he was going to explode, he pressed himself between her legs, trying to go slow, trying to resist the urge to shove forward and impale her with a single deep thrust.

But she put her hands on his chest, holding him back. Her eyes pierced his.

"Maximo," she whispered, "everyone I've ever loved has lied to me. If you're keeping anything from me, tell me now. Before I lose myself completely..."

Stroking her hair, he looked deeply into her eyes and lied to her. "*Proprio niente, cara.* There's nothing."

She smiled back at him for a brief instant, and joy filled her soft brown eyes. Then she gasped, arching her back as he pushed into her. She moaned, turning her head from side to side as he gripped her hips in his hands, penetrating her inch by inch. He sucked in his breath at the force of his pleasure. He'd never felt anything remotely like this. Shocked, he drew back, then thrust into her again. And again. And again, with increasing roughness.

Growling aloud, he held her hips tight, riding her hard until their bodies were hot with sweat. Her body began to coil with new tension beneath his touch.

"Don't…" she muttered, biting her tender pink lip. Her eyes were closed as she gave a shuddering intake of breath. "Don't stop. Please…oh God, please…"

Her dark hair was twisted and tangled around her naked shoulders. Every time he thrust into her, her breasts bounced softly. Her slender white hands gripped his hips now, unknowingly controlling his rhythm. She finally screamed, bucking her hips, and he thrust into her with a final explosive shout. He nearly blacked out from the pleasure as he poured his seed into her.

He collapsed next to her on the bed with a hoarse, exhausted sigh. Lying next to her on the bed, he held her. He tenderly kissed his wife's sweaty forehead. "Goddess," he whispered. "*Donna molto bella.* You're *mine.*"

But even as he murmured the words, he knew that if she ever found out the truth this would all come to a crashing end.

It was a new world.

Lucy had never known that sex could be like this.

This—this intoxicating drug was why people made

such fools of themselves for the sake of desire. She understood it now.

Her husband's skills exceeded even his Casanova legend. He was better than Heathcliff—better than Mr. Darcy. What he could do with his hands. What he could do with his *tongue*...

She blushed. Hours later, lying naked yet again in his arms, she ran her fingers along the edge of his strong, masculine hand, his dark-haired forearm. They'd made love three times today now. Twice before his aunt had returned with Chloe. They'd taken a brief break to have dinner—both of them had been starving, and he'd cooked for them as she played with her daughter—then they'd put Chloe to bed in her crib.

And Maximo had picked up Lucy in his arms and tossed her into the master bedroom next door.

She should have been exhausted. Spent. And yet she was strangely wired—too energized to even think of sleeping. She couldn't stop looking at him. She pressed her head against his shoulder, looking up at the sharp edge of his cheekbone, his masculine beauty.

Moonlight pooled on the foot of the bed, lining her dark sleeping prince with silver.

Sex without love. Was it possible?

For him, perhaps. Not for her.

She knew it for certain now. Because with his every kiss, his every thrust, she'd felt herself falling deeper.

Disaster. But there was nothing she could do. She couldn't pick and choose her feelings like Maximo could. She was falling in love with him. With a playboy prince who hated her grandfather, who'd married her only to get his revenge and who planned to casually divorce her, tossing her in the trash like stale bread.

She'd lost their war. Lost it completely. She would have only three months with him before she lost him forever. Before she lost the perfect husband and perfect father who had only one flaw—that he wanted to be neither a husband nor a father.

And of course there was that additional problem of him insisting that her grandfather die miserable and alone.

Her hand involuntarily clenched against his chest. Giuseppe Ferrazzi was a stranger to her, but he was still her family. She couldn't allow him to suffer. Not when she could do something about it.

She had to end the feud between the two men.

Not just for her grandfather's sake—but for Maximo's. She had to find out what demons haunted him. She had to find out what her grandfather had done. Only then could she end the feud and save them both...

Maximo covered her hand with his larger one. "Do you want more already, *cara*?" His voice was sleepy. Eyes still closed, he turned toward her, pulling her to nestle closer to his naked body. "I can see you're going to keep me very busy."

She took a deep breath. "Maximo? What did my grandfather do to your family?"

The lines of his face hardened and he started to roll away. "I don't wish to discuss it."

"No. Stop." She grabbed his bare shoulder. "We're going back to Aquillina tomorrow. If you don't tell me the story, I will hear it from him."

"No!"

"He's my grandfather, Maximo! Contract or no contract, you can't expect me to just leave him to die alone. Not without good reason!"

He stared at her, his eyes alight and terrible. Moonlight traced the whites of his eyes.

"*Bene, cara.* I'll tell you." His voice was low and dangerous. "The day you were born, there was a blizzard in Aquillina, the worst ever seen. My mother and sister became sick with pneumonia. We were living far from the village, in my aunt's old *pensione*. My father phoned Ferrazzi, asking him to send the only doctor from his villa."

"Go on," she said in a tiny voice.

"Ferrazzi refused to even give him the message. My father snapped on some old skis and set out for Aquillina to get him." His hand tightened around her. "But he never returned. He froze to death in the snow. And without the antibiotics my mother and sister needed, they died two days later."

She sucked in her breath. "Oh, Maximo."

"I promised my father I'd stay with my mother and sister. That I'd take care of them. But all I could do was watch them die."

"Maximo, I'm so sorry. I wish there was something I could do to take the pain away. I...I..."

She wanted to say *I love you*, but the words stuck in her throat. How could she say them when he'd warned her against ever loving him? What if he responded with anger, or worse—pity?

"I'm sorry," she repeated.

"You and your mother were both healthy and strong

after the birth. It was only selfishness that made Ferrazzi keep the doctor at his villa—selfishness and spite. He'd already ruined us, but it wasn't enough for him. The day I buried my family, I knew I would get my revenge. I would take everything from him. Everything."

She wrapped her arms around Maximo, trying desperately to offer comfort. He was her husband, and she loved him. All she wanted to do was comfort him.

He took a deep breath.

"In three days, we'll have a wedding. He will hear about it across the village—across the world. And he will realize the enormity of what he's lost. His company. His fortune. His place in society. And his granddaughter."

Maximo's voice was grim and cold. Troubled, she drew away. How had she fallen in love with a man like this—a man who was not only incapable of love, but who could be so vengeful and cruel?

"Go to sleep," he said, rolling over on his side. "We leave very early for Aquillina."

She stared at his dark figure in the shadows.

He's not incapable of love, she thought. She'd seen too much good in him to believe that. His anger and guilt over his family's loss had just festered in him like a sore, eating away at his soul.

Lucy thought of the old man sobbing in the street. Surely her grandfather had never meant to hurt Maximo's family. He'd only been trying to protect his own, by keeping the doctor for his daughter-in-law and newborn granddaughter…

Lucy had to end the feud between them.

If she could heal Maximo's pain, perhaps he could

open up his heart. He would see how much Lucy and Chloe both needed him. He might be able to love them. He might decide to make their family a real one…

You're dreaming, she told herself harshly. The playboy prince would never settle down. He would never love her.

But.

She could still love him.

Instead of saying those three little words aloud, she could show her love—by taking the pain out of his heart. Then even after he divorced her and forgot her very existence, she would at least know she'd done something to make his life better. To make him happy.

She listened to her husband's breathing slip into the evenness of sleep. Putting her hands behind her head, she stared at the ceiling. How could she make the men talk to each other? Where? She sucked in her breath.

The wedding. A joyous celebration, families united by love. What better time or place?

"For you, Maximo," she whispered without sound, speaking the words like a silent prayer in the darkness. "Because I love you."

CHAPTER FIFTEEN

THREE days later, Villa Uccello was in total wedding-day uproar.

"Let me in!" Maximo roared, pounding the bedroom door.

"No!" Lucy leaned back against it. Her teeth chattered with the reverberating force of his pounding. "It's bad luck for you to see me today!"

"Lucy, be reasonable! It's an evening wedding. You can't expect me not to see you all day long. This is torture!"

She covered a laugh. She could just *bet* he wanted to see her. Ever since they'd returned to Aquillina, they'd both been busy—he with wrapping up the details of the Ferrazzi acquisition, and Lucy with her planner trying to create her dream wedding in just a few short days.

Three days of dress-fittings and cake-tastings, with Chloe sampling as much frosting as she could get her chubby little hands on. Three days of being interviewed by reporters from around the world. Three days of manicures and pedicures and massages, as Maximo had brought the team of stylists from Milan to stay at the Villa Uccello at Lucy's beck and call. Three days of luxury and frantic fun, of feeling like a bride, of feeling like a star.

And three nights of unbridled passion in her husband's bed.

Every night, he set her world on fire. Even once in the middle of the afternoon, when he'd found her alone in the hallway and dragged her into a quiet unused study. He'd made love to her against a wall of leather-bound Italian books. She flushed hot to her toes. She would never think of Machiavelli or Petrarch in quite the same way again.

So it was no wonder he was so frustrated, Lucy thought, since it had now been ten hours since they'd last made love. She could understand why he might be going a little crazy.

So was she.

But she was pushing him away for a good cause. One that had nothing to do with wedding-day superstition.

This was her last chance to try to sneak away before the wedding. Her last chance to speak with Giuseppe Ferrazzi and find out his side of the story, so she could invite him to the celebration with a clear conscience. Once she was sure that their feud was all based on a misunderstanding, she would have no qualms about forcing the two men to meet in public. Maximo would never want to insult his dignity with a humiliating public scene. He would have no choice but to listen, if only for a few scant moments.

And she would end the feud between the men. She'd

save her grandfather from poverty and loneliness, and save the soul of the man she loved.

If Maximo could never love her, at least he might someday love *someone*. Thinking of him with another woman made her want to rip her heart out, but Maximo's happiness was everything to her.

Even if he couldn't be happy with her.

Maximo's pounding on the bedroom door increased.

"Cara—" he sounded truly desperate now "—have mercy! I'm just a man!"

"Maximo, go away!" she said over the lump in her throat. "It's for your own good!"

Growling and muttering in Italian, he left.

When she was sure he was gone, she took a deep breath, squared her shoulders and went to the nursery. Waking up Chloe from her morning nap, she bundled her against the cold, and grabbed a coat for herself.

She tiptoed them both past the enormous kitchen, where Ermanno was tucking into a plate of late-morning pasta. Over her objections, Maximo had recently assigned him to be her bodyguard. With his three hundred pounds of muscle and bulk, he'd be eating his lunch for an hour. And Georgiana Stewart, her British wedding planner, had ordered Lucy to take a refreshing nap ("just forty-five minutes to restore your skin's youthful glow, Princess"), warning the servants to leave both Lucy and her baby to sleep in peace.

Now all Lucy could do was cross her fingers and pray she was successful. And able to finish her mission before anyone, especially Maximo, caught her.

It was dangerous. For her to even talk to Giuseppe

was a breach of the prenuptial agreement. If Maximo decided to nullify their marriage contract, Lucy and her daughter would be left destitute.

But she had to risk it. She couldn't choose between her husband and her grandfather. She couldn't live happily with her baby, knowing that a mile away the poor old man was suffering alone. And she couldn't bear for Maximo to live his whole life suffering as well, choking on the vengeful guilt in his soul.

Not when she could fix everything.

She would protect all the people she loved. She would save them, even from themselves.

Maximo had good in his heart. She'd seen it. All the times he'd been good to her and Chloe without benefit to himself proved it.

Tucking Chloe into a stroller, she hurried through the villa's elaborate gardens. She waited until the security guard was distracted, flirting with a pretty reporter, then escaped behind the bushes near the back gate.

So far, so good. Lucy reached the edge of the village. The snow had long melted, the sun was warm and the days were already growing longer. Spring was just around the corner, lifting her spirits. Now if she could just find her grandfather's old villa without anyone noticing...

A foolish hope. Even if she weren't the *principessa*, the new darling of the whole village, the street was packed full of people trying to see her. The village was filled with florist and catering trucks, reporters covering the "single mother rags-to-riches" story and international paparazzi stalking the illustrious guests scheduled to arrive from the Villa d'Este, opened out-of-season especially for the event.

"La principessa!" she heard a voice shout down the street. Heart pounding, she ducked back into an alleyway between two old houses.

A kind-eyed, white-haired woman was at the end of the alley, sweeping with a broom. *"Bambina?"*

Lucy knew this woman. She struggled to remember the Italian word. *"Bambinaia?"*

The woman dropped the broom with a clatter. She burst into excited chatter in Italian, embracing first Lucy and then Chloe. She pulled them both into her tiny kitchen. Lucy knew that her old nanny didn't speak English, but the request she had to make didn't need translation.

Lucy pleaded, "Giuseppe Ferrazzi?"

For a long moment, the old woman stared at her. Then, with a reluctant sigh, she nodded.

Leaving the stroller behind, Lucy carried Chloe in her arms as she followed her old nanny through a web of alleyways in the back streets of the village. Beckoning her with a trembling hand, Annunziata suddenly pointed up. Her grandfather's villa.

"Grazie," she said, kissing the woman's cheek. She turned toward the door of the half-ruined villa, her heart singing with optimism and hope. She'd made it! She would speak to her grandfather, and hear his side of the story. Surely two proud men who had both lost so much could come to some peace.

"You're going to meet your great-grandfather," she told Chloe happily as she knocked on the door. "You'll see—it's all going to work out!"

But an hour later, Chloe was wailing unheeded in her

arms as Lucy looked at the old man in shock. Cold tea had been left untasted on the table as she tried to comprehend what he'd just told her.

"No," she whispered. "Maximo didn't do that. He wouldn't."

Her grandfather gripped the faded gold-painted arms of his antique chair. His raspy voice had a heavy accent. "So you see why you must help me destroy him."

"Destroy him?" she repeated numbly. She thought of the times Maximo had been kind to her. He'd saved her from Darryl in Chicago. Comforted her after she saw Alex in Rome. He'd carried her across the field of flowers, kissing her beneath the hot Sicilian sun.

The images stabbed at her like a knife.

He hadn't done it out of some hidden spark of good in his soul. He'd done it out of guilt. Bone-crushing, hellish *guilt*.

Abruptly the sound of her daughter's crying cut through her thoughts, focusing her. "Shh, baby, shh." She held Chloe close, snuggling her, breathing in her baby scent. Her daughter was soon comforted, but who would ever comfort Lucy…ever again?

"Have no fear, *mia nipotina*." Her grandfather's rheumy eyes were bright and wild. "We will get vengeance."

Vengeance? Her mother hadn't raised her to be so heartless. "No," she said faintly. "That's not what I want."

"You will listen to me. I am your grandfather," he demanded. "You will do as I say—"

"No." She rose abruptly from the chair. "I will do as I think best."

Vengeance wasn't what she wanted.

But justice…

She recalled Amelia pleading with her the first day they'd arrived in Aquillina, begging her not to humiliate Maximo in front of the village, begging her to keep their quarrels private. But privacy had been her undoing. Maximo had charmed away her suspicions and fears beneath the force of his arrogance and strength…and unexpected kindness.

A prince. A handsome prince.

Coming for her. Saving her. Taking care of her and Chloe forever. Teaching Lucy to feel again. To be brave. To risk her battered heart one last time.

She'd known all along it was too good to be true.

She closed her eyes, took a deep breath. When she exhaled, all her hopes and dreams left her body with the breath.

Leaving room for only one thing.

The truth.

She lifted her chin.

"I'll make Maximo confess," she said. "Tonight, at the wedding, he will admit…to everything."

CHAPTER SIXTEEN

MAXIMO gasped when he saw her.

His princess stood at the other end of the aisle. Lucy's dark hair was pulled back beneath a veil, held in place by the priceless diamond tiara that matched the necklace at her throat. Her white gown had long, form-fitting sleeves and a tight corset bodice that exploded into a frothy, wide skirt. Her red lipstick emphasized her full mouth, and the color matched the long-stemmed scarlet roses in her hand.

As if of one accord, the wedding guests rose to their feet with an appreciative gasp. Scores of the world's rich and famous were packed into the tiny private chapel. But even the jaded movie stars, princes and prime ministers, politicians and billionaires were in awe.

Lucy appeared like a vision in the ancient chapel, lit by hundreds of candles on the cold, wintry night, bedecked by roses red as blood.

Goddess of winter, he thought with a lump in his throat. *Donna molto bella*. So beautiful it made him hurt to look at her.

Lucy.

Staring at her was like staring at the sun, and Maximo couldn't take his eyes away from her.

What had he done, what had he ever done in his whole life, to deserve her as his wife?

Fate had forgiven him.

He needed no other proof than this. He'd never known another woman like Lucy. So beautiful, so loving, with such a pure heart. She'd made him see how rich and deep his world could really be. She was his partner—his equal in every way. *No*, he thought suddenly. Not his equal. She was more than that.

She was his heart.

I love her, he realized in shock.

He didn't just want to make love to her every night. He wanted to wake up to her every day for the rest of his life. He wanted to possess her forever. And more...

He wanted her to possess him.

Dio santo, he loved her!

He'd never felt like this before. Never even imagined that he could. His princess. His bride.

Lucy. He stared at her, willing her to look at him, trying to show in his eyes all the love he felt in his heart. *Lucy, ti amo.*

He'd married her to get his hands on Ferrazzi—to get control of the company and his revenge on the old man. He'd married her to end his old guilt, to give her the security she'd lost as a baby.

But a miracle had occurred—he loved her.

He, who'd never been caught by any woman, who'd never once experienced a broken heart, was utterly captivated by his wife.

Ti amo, Lucy.

But she wouldn't meet his gaze. And the longer he looked at her, he realized that something was wrong. Very, very wrong. Why wouldn't she meet his gaze?

Non è niente di grave, he tried to convince himself. *It is nothing. The flicker of the candles—the angle of her veil—they cause shadows.*

He'd spoken with her just that morning. He remembered the warmth of her voice as she'd scolded him through the door. What could have changed since then?

Then, for the first time, he saw the man behind her. Hanging over her like a wraith.

Giuseppe Ferrazzi.

Hatred ripped through him so great and powerful that he couldn't move.

How had Ferrazzi reached her? In spite of all his bodyguards? In spite of everything?

They came down the short aisle. As the audience sat back down, still murmuring appreciatively over the stunning beauty of the bride, they had no idea of what they were about to witness.

But the villagers in the back of the chapel knew. He saw their stunned faces, their wide eyes. Amelia, holding a slumbering Chloe in the front row, had a face as white as snow.

How…? How was it possible?

There could be only one explanation. Lucy had defied him. Ignoring his orders, she'd risked everything, going behind Maximo's back to visit the old man.

Leaving only one grim question.

What had Ferrazzi told her?

As Lucy finally arrived by his side, he gently reached over and lifted her veil. He looked into her beautiful face, and knew the answer.

Ferrazzi had told her *everything*.

All the light had gone out of her expressive brown eyes. All the warmth. And it wasn't until now, when it was gone, that he realized that it was her light which had kept him warm since the day he'd plucked her from the gas station in Chicago and forced her to become his bride.

He'd meant to save her.

But she was the one who'd saved him, from a cold life of vengeance and empty pleasures.

Why had she spoken to Ferrazzi, today of all days? Why, when they could have been so happy?

"Why did you do it?" he said in a low voice, for her alone. "Why did you defy me?"

She didn't look at him. Her voice was hollow. "Because I loved you."

Loved. Past tense.

The priest began the ceremony, speaking first in Italian, then in English. Ignoring the man, ignoring the eighty guests watching them, Maximo grabbed his bride's shoulders. He stared down into her tearstained face. "Lucy."

Defiantly she looked toward the chapel's dark windows. He wanted her—not just her body but her soul—in a way that made him catch his breath. He wanted her to look at him as she had just yesterday. He hadn't realized until now just how truly happy they'd been...

"Lucy, look at me."

"No." Candlelight flickered against the cold beauty of her face.

"Look at me!" he thundered.

Lucy turned, and her brown eyes blazed.

"Why?" she cried. "So you can use your charm to make me forget that you kidnapped me as baby? *That you murdered my parents?*"

The whole chapel was suddenly quiet as a forgotten grave. From a distance, he could hear water dripping from melting icicles outside, hear the cold wind howling across the lake.

Standing behind her, Giuseppe Ferrazzi glared at him with bright, beady eyes. This was his final vengeance. The dying old man didn't care whose life he ruined, even his granddaughter's. If he couldn't have his old life back, with his power and money and family, then he wanted retribution at any price.

Exactly how Maximo had been before he'd fallen in love with Lucy.

"*Cara, per favore.*" His hand tightened around her shoulder. "If I could speak with you alone—"

"No," she said in a choked voice. She pulled her arm away. "You lied to me. All this time, I knew—I knew!—that there was some other reason you were being so good and kind." She shook her head, and tears spilled over her lashes. "It just never occurred to me it was because you were racked with guilt."

"Let's go talk—"

"No!" She stepped back as he tried to reach for her. "Here and now, Maximo. Tell me the truth."

He looked around the chapel, at his friends, his business rivals, people he admired and respected from around the globe. They all watched the scene with fascinated horror. The photographers in the back were wildly snapping pictures. The society wedding of the season had just turned into a garish tragedy that would sell even more papers than before.

The humiliation and shame of this moment washed over him. He wanted to lash out. Shout his frustration. Mostly he wanted to punch the old man in the face.

But he did not.

Because of *her*. This was his chance. His only precious chance to fight for the only woman he'd ever loved.

If this was to be the place, so be it.

Tightening his hands into fists, he raised his chin.

"I never hurt your parents," he said quietly. "They were already dead when I found their car at the bottom of the cliff. Your grandfather never believed that, but it is the truth. The truth," he repeated in a hard voice, looking at Ferrazzi over Lucy's head. "When your men beat me for two days afterward, you were trying to make me confess to something I didn't do. *They were already dead.*"

"You beat him for two days?" Lucy whirled to face the old man. "He was just a child!"

Ferrazzi didn't even look at her. His lip curled. "My only mistake was in letting you go, D'Aquilla," he rasped, "so you could grow up and take my company from me. I should have dumped you in the lake in a weighted sack!"

Lucy sucked in her breath, looking between them. "Monsters," she whispered. "You're both monsters. And I don't want any part of you. Either of you!"

She turned to go. Maximo stopped her, blocking her from the aisle.

"Please. Don't go."

"Why?"

"You've always asked me for the truth. The truth is, Lucy…" He took a deep breath. "I love you."

"You…you what?"

"I love you," he said quietly. *"Ti amo."*

"Admit what you did to me," she whispered. "I want to hear it from your lips."

He closed his eyes.

Then he looked into her face and told her the truth.

"I heard the car go off the cliff. I heard the crunch of metal as it hit. I rushed toward the car, and heard a baby crying. I pulled you out of the car before it exploded."

Her eyes widened imperceptibly. "So you're saying…you saved me?"

He wished he could be so noble. He shook his head. "When I took you from the car, I knew it was my chance for revenge at last. There was an American woman staying at my aunt's *pensione*. She'd said she was desperate for a child. So I…gave her one."

"That's how you knew I was in Illinois," she said. Unshed tears shone from her eyes. "All these years, you've known I was alive. But you let me be neglected in foster care, forgotten until you found another selfish use for me."

"No, Lucy, no!" He shook his head vehemently. "I realized my mistake long ago. I wouldn't wish my greatest enemy to be raised by a man like Ferrazzi—" he gave the man a hard look "—but I tried to find you. But your mother just disappeared. Changed her profession. Even changed her name. I couldn't find you. Until

I looked into Wentworth's past for something to use against him...and found you. It was fate, *cara*," he whispered, reaching out to stroke her dark hair. *"Il destino."*

"Fate." Her beautiful red lips curled. "I asked you for the truth. Begged you. And you lied to me. Your kisses, comforts, sweet words—all lies."

"No—not a lie. I just didn't tell you everything." He moved toward her in the candlelight, desperate to touch her, to caress her cheek, to make her understand. "At first there didn't seem any point, and later, I was afraid—"

"You. Lied." She backed away, hurt and anger and confusion mixing in her expression. "Alexander only took a year from me. You took my whole childhood. And you made me love you," she whispered. "I'll never forgive you for that."

She started to turn away.

"Marry me."

She stopped, whirling to face him. "What?"

The ache in his throat was so great that he could barely summon his old bravado, his old charm. But he tried like hell.

"Let me make it up to you." He held up the priceless eight-carat diamond ring set in platinum. "I will never keep another secret from you. I will spend the rest of my life trying to make you happy. Not because of what you own, but because of who you are. I love you, *cara*. Stay with me. Be my wife forever."

Furrowing her brow in hurt and confusion, she gasped, "My God, is there anything you won't lie about in order to win?"

"I'm not lying!" In front of the whole roomful of

people, Prince Maximo d'Aquilla allowed himself to reveal his vulnerability. Every muscle in his body was tense as he held the ring out to her, hardly daring to breathe. "I'm asking you to love me. I'm asking you to be mine."

Slowly she took the ring from him. She looked at the endlessly sparkling facets, the cold shine of the perfect diamond.

Va bene, he thought suddenly. *She's going to forgive. I will spend the rest of my life loving her...*

"You really love me?" she said softly.

"Yes!" he nearly shouted.

She closed her eyes and took a deep breath. When she opened her eyes, they were as cold as the old man's.

"Good," she said. "Then this will hurt."

She threw the enormous diamond ring at his face, drawing blood on his cheek where the prongs scraped against his skin.

The crowd gasped.

Touching the drops of blood, Maximo watched as she turned on her heel. Snatching up her sleeping child in her arms, Lucy fled the chapel in a swirl of frothy silk and tulle. He heard a single sob as she disappeared, echoing like a swan's plaintive cry across the lake.

"Now," he heard Giuseppe Ferrazzi say with satisfaction behind him, "I can die a happy man."

CHAPTER SEVENTEEN

HALFWAY on the drive to Milan, Chloe woke up crying for her purple hippo, and Lucy realized to her horror that she'd left it behind.

She'd been so rushed when she left the villa, so desperate to get out before Maximo could follow her and convince her to stay, before he could repeat the lie that he loved her. Love her? He would never love her. It had just been his last, heartless attempt to beat her grandfather.

Leaving her wedding dress and the priceless diamonds on their bed—the bed where they'd been so happy together—she'd packed a few items of clothing for herself and Chloe. And her three Ferrazzi handbags. She no longer wanted the thirty million her husband promised her. Let Maximo and Giuseppe fight over her family company till doomsday; she didn't want it. She was going back to Chicago where things made sense.

But things were going to be different this time.

Her alligator satchel would be worth thousands of dollars even on the secondhand market. That would be enough to pay her back rent and set up a small nest egg for emergencies.

And she wouldn't get her job back at the gas station. She would fight for the promotion she'd earned. Once she went to the H.R. department of the gas station chain and explained what had happened with Darryl, she knew she could convince them to still make her the assistant manager of a different store. Then she would start taking night classes. It might take a few years, studying at night while Chloe slept, but she would get her college degree. She'd be a school librarian and teach kids to love books as she'd dreamed.

Lucy had once thought that being a mother meant she had to give up her own dreams. But in the last few weeks, she'd learned that wasn't true. Fairy tales could happen at any age. It was never too late to dream— never too late to achieve anything she was willing to work for.

Except for one dream. That was lost forever.

The dream of loving Maximo.

Even after she'd realized she'd left the purple hippo behind, she hadn't been able to go back and face the man who'd lied to her and broken her heart. Pressing on the gas, she'd cried with her baby all the way to the airport in Milan. Then using five different credit cards, she bought a plane ticket to Chicago.

She'd checked their suitcase, passed security and found a dark, deserted waiting area. It was the middle of the night when she tried to settle Chloe down to sleep on a reclining chair. As they waited for their early morning flight, the airport's hallways became deserted and most of the shops closed. Other than an occasional announcement over the loudspeaker, it was soon quiet.

Except for the crying baby.

Chloe wouldn't sleep. And she wouldn't stop crying. Tears shone on her plump cheeks, and her little body was racked with sobs.

"Shh, Chloe, shh." Lucy snuggled her close, trying to comfort her. But it was all she could do not to wail along with her baby.

She'd tried so hard not to love Maximo. So hard. But he'd made it impossible. She'd thought him so strong, so tender, so powerful. So wonderful. But he'd ruined Lucy's whole life by taking her from her family as a baby.

Did that really ruin your life? the thought whispered in her mind.

Of course it did! she replied furiously, then stopped.

As a heartbroken, angry boy of twelve, Maximo had saved her from a fire. He'd taken her to be raised by Connie Abbott, a warm, wonderful woman who'd loved her. Read her stories. Baked her cookies. Kissed away her fears. Taught her about integrity and hard work and love.

How different would her life have been if she'd been raised by a cold, vengeful man like Giuseppe Ferrazzi?

It doesn't matter, she told herself angrily. Maximo had lied to her. He'd lured her into his bed by playing recklessly with her heart. And worst of all: he'd even tried to claim he loved her!

The playboy prince would never love anyone. He'd only said that to try to hold on to his victory against Giuseppe, to beat the old man he hated.

"Monsters," she whispered aloud. Thank God she'd gotten them away from Maximo before Chloe was too attached. Before they were both too happy. Before…

She burst into tears.

"Principessa."

Surprised, Chloe abruptly stopped wailing. Lucy looked up and saw Ermanno, her ex-bodyguard, standing next to Maximo's pilot. Wiping her eyes, she glanced around in fear that their boss might be nearby. "What do you want? How did you find me?"

"A *paparazzo* followed you to the airport. The prince asked me to offer my assistance." The Australian pilot bowed his head respectfully. "I am to give you a ride to anywhere you wish to go."

"And this is for you." Ermanno held out a manila envelope.

"What is it?"

He gave an expressive Italian shrug.

She opened the envelope. It contained the information for a numbered Swiss bank account.

And then she saw the amount.

"I don't understand," she whispered.

"There's a note," he said.

Fearing what she would find, she reached back into the envelope. There was indeed a short note in Maximo's handwriting.

I've deposited the payment agreed upon per our contract into your account. Thirty million dollars, plus the current full market value for Ferrazzi SpA, equals three hundred million.

Thank you for being so good to me. I never deserved you. I'll never forget you. My wife. My love. The only one.

It was unsigned. Sucking in her breath, Lucy held the paper close. "Where is he?"

"Gone," the pilot said. "I flew him to Rome as he wished to transfer Ferrazzi to your grandfather. Then he wanted to get away—"

"He gave away Ferrazzi?" she gasped. "To my *grandfather*?"

The pilot nodded. "I saw Signor Ferrazzi in Rome. Looking hale and hearty, too, I might add. Apparently he himself started the rumor that he was dying." He shook his head. "Makes me glad I'm a pilot and not part of the fashion business."

Ermanno suddenly hit his forehead. "*Mi scusi, principessa*. The prince, he asked me to give you this at once, the instant I saw you. He said you'd be wanting it far more than money. Here it is—"

And from the pocket of his voluminous leather coat, he pulled out a ragged purple lump. Chloe saw it and clapped her hands with a delighted gasp.

A sob rose to Lucy's lips.

Hippo.

Maximo had found Hippo and knew what it meant to Chloe. He'd saved her. Just as he'd saved Lucy in Chicago.

He hadn't ruined their lives. He'd taken care of them both. Protected them from Alex. Treated Chloe like his own daughter. Showered affection and gifts. Cooked for them. Read books to Chloe. And seduced Lucy with pleasure she'd never imagined possible. And at the end, even after she'd left him, he'd given up Ferrazzi—the hard-won prize he'd sought for twenty years.

Why would he do that?

There was only one explanation. Maximo hadn't been pretending.

He really did love her.

He loved her, and she'd humiliated him. Thrown the ring back in his face. Drawn his blood in front of the whole world.

Who was really the monster?

With a harsh intake of breath, Lucy leaped to her feet. Chloe was too rapturous over Hippo to give more than a squawk of protest as Lucy turned fiercely to the pilot.

"Where is he?"

The pilot looked startled. "The prince does not wish anyone to know, your highness."

"Tell me right now!" She stepped toward him, feeling like she might do something desperate. "Tell me!"

The pilot shook his head sorrowfully. "I'm sorry. He expressly ordered me to tell no one."

Lucy wanted to shake him, but what good would that do? It wasn't the pilot's fault. The man was only following orders. Exhausted, choked with grief, she covered her face with her hand.

She'd been such a fool. She'd had Maximo's love, and she'd thrown it all away. And now it was too late. She'd lost him.

Her former bodyguard suddenly turned his three-hundred-pound bulk on the pilot.

"Tell her," he growled.

She looked up with an intake of breath.

"I can't," the skinny pilot told him, looking startled. "The paparazzi are vultures. One whisper and it all gets out. He wants to be left in peace. I gave him my word."

"Fine. Don't tell her a thing," Ermanno said. He cracked his knuckles. "Just fly her to wherever he is."

"Well, I—" The pilot hesitated, looking from Ermanno to Lucy to Chloe. Then slowly he sighed. "All right, Princess. I cannot resist true love."

CHAPTER EIGHTEEN

THE World's Most Eligible Bachelor Rejected! Handsome Prince Spurned Amid Accusations of Long-Ago Crime, the headline read.

"Serves him right," said heartbroken former girlfriend Esmé Landon, the countess of Bedingford. "He's dished it out for long enough—about time he had to take it!"

The day after he lost the love of his life, it was still sinking in. Maximo stared down at the tabloid in his hands, feeling a lump in his throat.

So this was what heartache felt like.

All these years he'd been a playboy, casually breaking hearts right and left, and he'd never known...

"You shouldn't read that trash," his aunt Silvana said sharply behind him in Italian.

"I'm not." He crumpled the paper in his hands and tossed it in the fire. "It's kindling."

She nodded with an expressive snort and flare of nostril. "I will make you some lunch."

"I'm not hungry. Go home, Silvana. You have your own life."

"Of course I do," she replied, tucking back her white hair, bright as snow against her smooth, youthful skin. "But I've canceled my afternoon date. You're my priority today."

He gaped at her. "A date?"

She gave him a smile that managed to be both impish—and serene. "Don't worry about that." She made a *tsk*ing sound as she searched the cabinets. "But this kitchen is empty! I'm going back to my house to make you a proper meal. I will send Amelia with some pasta." She shook her umbrella at him threateningly. "And you'd better eat it!"

He was in no mood to eat. "No. I mean it."

But his aunt had already left. He sank down onto the rough wooden floor, staring at the fire. Outside, rain was pouring, and the whole cottage seemed to shiver beneath the weight of the storm.

He should have told Lucy the truth all along.

Now he'd lost her. Because he hadn't been honest with her from the very beginning. He'd thought, if he tried hard enough, he could hold it all together without giving her the one thing that she kept demanding—the truth...

Maximo held his head in his hands. He'd always been so strong, but losing her had taken that. After twenty years, fate had finally found a way to make him pay for his crime of stealing Lucy from her rightful family.

He whirled around at a noise. "*Zia*, I told you, I'm not hungry—"

But it wasn't his aunt.

Lucy stood in the doorway, soaking wet from the rain.

He leaped to his feet. He didn't speak. He didn't pause. He just went straight to her and pulled her into his arms. He held her tightly against his heart.

Then he kissed her.

"Maximo," Lucy whispered as he pulled away. "I'm so sorry."

"You're sorry?" he said incredulously. "I'm the one who hurt you. I took you from your family. You asked me for the truth and I lied. I thought that if I spent the rest of my life making it up to you, it would be enough. You have to know how desperately I regret—"

She stopped him with a finger to his lips.

"Words are cheap. I learned that from Alex." Tears mingled with the rain on her skin. She reached up to stroke his rough cheek. "You showed your love for us with your actions again and again. Why did you do it, Maximo?" Her expressive brown eyes glistened. "Why did you pay me full market value for my shares, when you'd already given the company back to my grandfather? How could you give that away?"

"Having the company didn't bring my family back to me." He shook his head, suddenly feeling damnably close to crying himself. "I don't care about hurting Ferrazzi anymore. I just want you, Lucy. You and Chloe are my family now. I would do anything for you. I would give up my quest for revenge, I would give up my fortune. I would die for you."

"I know." She held him tightly. "I know."

Long minutes later, he looked up. "Where's our daughter?"

"Still sleeping in the car with Amelia. I found your

cousin walking outside in the rain. Chloe was so tired. She wouldn't fall asleep until she had her hippo in her arms." She swallowed. "Until she knew we were coming home to you."

"Can you really forgive what I did?" he whispered. "You deserved a family. And I took that away from you."

"No. You gave me a mother." Placing her small hands beneath his chin, she forced him to meet her gaze. "Connie Abbott loved me. I am the person I am today because of her. And...because of you."

"Lucy." He could barely speak over the lump in his throat.

Rising on her tiptoes, she kissed him. The patter of rain against the roof slowed, then stopped. Her kiss was gentle, tender, promising a lifetime of trust and a whole heart.

The kiss of his life, from the only woman he'd ever loved. The only woman he would ever love.

"Oh, no," they heard Amelia groan. "Chloe, don't look!"

Reluctantly they pulled away from their embrace. Fragile sunshine flooded through the doorway where Amelia stood, covering the baby's face with her hand. She rolled her eyes like the teenager she was.

"Your parents." Amelia sighed sympathetically to the baby as Chloe playfully pushed her hand away. "Won't they ever stop with the mushy stuff?"

Lucy leaned back against her husband as she stretched her arms up around his neck. "What do you think, *caro*? Will we ever stop?"

He looked down at her, loving her so much that it

suffused his whole being, making him feel like he was shining with it—so proud and tall and high that he could fly.

"I will love you as long as Sicily rises from the sea," he swore. "You and only you. I will love you until the stars cease to shine. Until—"

But at this moment, his bride turned around in his arms. "Show me?" she suggested shyly.

So he showed her, with a single kiss, how their love would last forever.

HIRED: FOR THE BOSS'S PLEASURE

She's gone from personal assistant
to mistress—but now he's demanding
she become the boss's bride!

Read all our fabulous stories this month:

MISTRESS: HIRED FOR THE BILLIONAIRE'S PLEASURE
by INDIA GREY

THE BILLIONAIRE BOSS'S INNOCENT BRIDE
by LINDSAY ARMSTRONG

HER RUTHLESS ITALIAN BOSS
by CHRISTINA HOLLIS

MEDITERRANEAN BOSS, CONVENIENT MISTRESS
by KATHRYN ROSS

HPE0209

REQUEST YOUR FREE BOOKS!

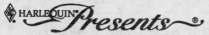 HARLEQUIN *Presents*

2 FREE NOVELS PLUS 2 FREE GIFTS!

YES! Please send me 2 FREE Harlequin Presents® novels and my 2 FREE gifts (gifts are worth about $10). After receiving them, if I don't wish to receive any more books, I can return the shipping statement marked "cancel". If I don't cancel, I will receive 6 brand-new novels every month and be billed just $4.05 per book in the U.S. or $4.74 per book in Canada, plus 25¢ shipping and handling per book and applicable taxes, if any*. That's a savings of close to 15% off the cover price! I understand that accepting the 2 free books and gifts places me under no obligation to buy anything. I can always return a shipment and cancel at any time. Even if I never buy another book, the two free books and gifts are mine to keep forever.

106 HDN ERRW   306 HDN ERRL

Name _____ (PLEASE PRINT)

Address _____ Apt. #

City _____ State/Prov. _____ Zip/Postal Code

Signature (if under 18, a parent or guardian must sign)

Mail to the **Harlequin Reader Service**:
IN U.S.A.: P.O. Box 1867, Buffalo, NY 14240-1867
IN CANADA: P.O. Box 609, Fort Erie, Ontario L2A 5X3

Not valid to current subscribers of Harlequin Presents books.

Want to try two free books from another line?
Call 1-800-873-8635 or visit www.morefreebooks.com.

* Terms and prices subject to change without notice. N.Y. residents add applicable sales tax. Canadian residents will be charged applicable provincial taxes and GST. Offer not valid in Quebec. This offer is limited to one order per household. All orders subject to approval. Credit or debit balances in a customer's account(s) may be offset by any other outstanding balance owed by or to the customer. Please allow 4 to 6 weeks for delivery. Offer available while quantities last.

Your Privacy: Harlequin Books is committed to protecting your privacy. Our Privacy Policy is available online at www.eHarlequin.com or upon request from the Reader Service. From time to time we make our lists of customers available to reputable third parties who may have a product or service of interest to you. If you would prefer we not share your name and address, please check here. ☐

HP08R

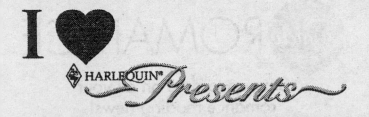

I ♥ HARLEQUIN® Presents

BROUGHT TO YOU BY FANS OF
HARLEQUIN PRESENTS.

We are its editors and authors
and biggest fans—and we'd
love to hear from YOU!

Subscribe today to our online blog at
www.iheartpresents.com

HARLEQUIN *Presents*

International Billionaires

Life is a game of power and pleasure.
And these men play to win!

Let Harlequin Presents® take you on a jet-set journey
to meet eight male wonders of the world. From rich
tycoons to royal playboys— they're red-hot and ruthless!

International Billionaires coming in 2009

THE PRINCE'S WAITRESS WIFE
by *Sarah Morgan*, February

AT THE ARGENTINEAN BILLIONAIRE'S BIDDING
by *India Grey*, March

THE FRENCH TYCOON'S PREGNANT MISTRESS
by *Abby Green*, April

THE RUTHLESS BILLIONAIRE'S VIRGIN
by *Susan Stephens*, May

THE ITALIAN COUNT'S DEFIANT BRIDE
by *Catherine George*, June

THE SHEIKH'S LOVE-CHILD
by *Kate Hewitt*, July

BLACKMAILED INTO THE GREEK TYCOON'S BED
by *Carol Marinelli*, August

THE VIRGIN SECRETARY'S IMPOSSIBLE BOSS
by *Carol Mortimer*, September

8 volumes in all to collect!

www.eHarlequin.com

HP12798

HARLEQUIN *Presents*

kept for his *Pleasure*

She's his mistress on demand!

Wherever seduction takes place, these fabulously
wealthy, charismatic, sexy men know how to
keep a woman coming back for more!

She's his mistress on demand—but when he
wants her body *and soul* he will be demanding
a whole lot more! Dare we say it…even marriage!

CONFESSIONS OF A MILLIONAIRE'S MISTRESS
by Robyn Grady

**Don't miss any books in
this exciting new miniseries
from Harlequin Presents!**

www.eHarlequin.com   HP12801